WHAT THE **RED** TIDE RAISES

ALCHEMY FURNACE

Matt Beside The Gardens

What the Red Tide Raises
Copyright © 2021 by Matt Beside The Gardens
mattbesidethegardens@protonmail.com

All rights reserved. No part of this publication may be reproduced, distributed, or transmitted in any form or by any means, including photocopying, recording, or other electronic or mechanical methods, without the prior written permission of the author, except in the case of brief quotations embodied in critical reviews and certain other non-commercial uses permitted by copyright law.

Tellwell Talent
www.tellwell.ca

ISBN
978-0-2288-5210-0 (Hardcover)
978-0-2288-5209-4 (Paperback)
978-0-2288-5211-7 (eBook)

Special thanks to Red Peony

Cover illustration:
Duong Minh Loc
locduongminh@gmail.com

Back cover illustration:
Wattana Bo
rainlantern@yahoo.com

This book, first in a series, and the books that follow, are presented in the format of a television script. To understand basic screenplay vocabulary, we suggest you use the links below or the following words in a search engine: Glossary Screenwriting Terms

http://www.movieoutline.com/articles/a-glossary-of-screenwriting-terms-and-filmmakingdefinitions.html

https://kb.finaldraft.com/s/article/Glossary-of-Screenwriting-Terms

"ALCHEMY FURNACE" (PILOT)

COLD OPEN

MONTAGE - VIDEO FOOTAGE OF TV NEWS AND NEWSPAPER ARTICLES EXPOSING HOW CHINA HAS BEEN A THREAT TO THE WEST FROM THE 1950s TO TODAY, UNFOLDING FASTER AND FASTER - FORMING HIGHER AND HIGHER PILES. THERE IS ALSO AN INDICATION THAT THESE FILES ARE IN THE PROCESS OF PERMANENT DELETION.

EXT. FOREST - DAY

TITLE: Pingtang, Guizhou Province, Southwestern China, 2002

In a densely vegetated area of a high mountain valley, two Chinese photographers, near each other, take pictures.

In a split second, they separate and go in different directions.

PHOTOGRAPHER 1 suddenly falls into a narrow gap between two cliffs.

PHOTOGRAPHER 2 hears the fall and becomes confused about the direction to take in order to rescue his friend.

                    PHOTOGRAPHER 2
                (in Chinese, shouting)
            Where are you?

Photographer 1 regains consciousness.

He frantically looks at his camera to
see if it has any damage.

While inspecting it carefully, bit
by bit, his eyes pass swiftly over
his injuries, some minor, others more
serious.

Suddenly, while inhaling sharply, he
looks in front of him and sees some
Chinese characters carved in the stone.

INSERT - (IN CHINESE) THE CHINESE
COMMUNIST PARTY PERISHES

                    DR PATTERSON (O.S.)
                Experts have estimated that
                this "hidden words stone" is
                270 million years old, dating
                from the Permian period.

BACK TO PRESENT

INT. LECTURE HALL - NIGHT

Dr Patterson, salt and pepper beard, a
classy mid 50s gentleman, is in a state
of exhaustion.

Standing alone on stage, the confident but fragile erudite is amidst the last leg of his lecture.

Every seat in the lecture hall is taken, judging by the shadows cast by the audience.

>DR PATTERSON
>So if the Chinese Communist Party (CCP) is about to "perish" at one point, how low would it need to go in order to set in motion the beginning of its demise? Well, with the CCP, the problem is that it always pushes further and further to the lowest denominator of wickedness. But one thing is sure, when the CCP hits rock bottom, it may have already dragged the whole world down with it.

For a second, Dr Patterson wipes the sweat off his face with a handkerchief, which he puts back in his jacket pocket.

He turns his head slightly to his left as he perceives some movement backstage.

>DR PATTERSON (CONT'D)
>China has been morally bankrupt since the 1930s and has continued to sink into

unmatchable inhumanity since recorded history. It was the CCP coronavirus bioweapon of 2019 that brought most of us to that conclusion. Others have noticed that the significant changes started around 1949 when communism took over.

He takes a quick look at his smart watch, which shows a timer set at 3 minutes and counting.

Another screen appears that warns him that his heartbeat is accelerating.

          DR PATTERSON (CONT'D)
The CCP went from enslaving multiple layers of the population, using all sorts of insane forms of torture that was used throughout history to, more recently, ripping live organs from prisoners of conscience for billions of dollars in profits annually. They were also caught killing and then plastinating the bodies of members of the same prisoners of conscience for a well-known international exhibition. But these atrocities are only the tip of the iceberg, it is merely the

> external, superficial expression
> of seismic degeneracy. It is
> far worse than that. I will
> elaborate now. Most of us
> hearing about these acts of
> inhuman cruelty for the first
> time are unmoved by these
> words. This is it! We have
> slowly become insensitive to
> extreme horror, but also to
> breathtaking beauty, thanks to
> socialist/communist ideology
> permeating the world for
> decades, including in our
> country. The Cold War never
> stopped. It has insidiously
> continued to covertly cause
> immeasurable damage.

Again, he seems distracted by something in the back of the lecture hall.

Suddenly, two glowing red dots appear - two red eyes that are staring at him.

> DR PATTERSON (CONT'D)
> How can you know that
> humankind has almost hit rock
> bottom? Some could argue that
> a civilization begins to rot
> when righteous religions fall.
> Others, who wouldn't dare go
> that far, only point out that
> it happens when intrinsic
> traditional values are

abandoned and society begins to decay and spoil.
(beat)
In 1999, three of mankind's basic values were under siege in China: Truth.
(beat)
Compassion.
(beat)
Tolerance.
(beat)
These are at the core of the meditation/spiritual practice Falun Gong, also called Falun Dafa. From that point on, at lightning speed, the CCP anti-values of Lies-Hate-Weakness spread epidemically like never before throughout China. And as China spread its pollution around the globe, the specter of communism brought most nations to the brink of moral collapse.

For a few seconds, Dr Patterson switches focus to his hands, which are shaking.

He looks up and starts the conclusion of his lecture.

DR PATTERSON (CONT'D)
Most of you are aware that this final act wouldn't have been possible without the

intervention of Mao in the 50s and 60s as he almost succeeded in wiping out 5,000 years of Chinese culture. The building blocks of all humanity were almost dealt a fatal blow. Many of you may recall the work of The Monument Men. They considered the slaughter of human culture through art almost worse than taking human life.
   (beat)
I will close my talk by referencing the insect kingdom. Albert Einstein said that if bees were to disappear, man would only have four years left to live. You and I have started finding dead bees on the sidewalks, in larger numbers every day. The life expectancy of a beehive without its queen is around 30 days. Then how much time do we have left in this world if the "queen of values and culture" is dying?
   (beat)
Thank you.

End of Dr Patterson's lecture. He looks at the timer on his watch and manually stops the countdown at 00:00:11.

As the red eyes in the back of the lecture hall move forward, clapping hands, slow and loud can be heard.

A moment later, a light appears at the back of the main aisle. It focuses on and follows MO HONG LONG, a somber-faced Chinese male, mid-60s, with the self-confidence to conceal ten thousand crimes under his massively decorated army uniform.

He removes his night vision googles and hooks them on his belt.

He walks toward Dr Patterson and stops in the middle of the aisle.

>> DR PATTERSON (CONT'D)
> (troubled)
> Chairman Mo Hong Long...

>> MO HONG LONG
> (in perfect English, enthusiastic)
> I'm knocked out by your performance! Better than the first time I heard you. As requested, you've delivered your lecture in less time than usual. Now, I'll hold up my end of the bargain...

A spotlight shines on Dr Patterson's wife and three children, on the left side of the stage.

Red guards remove the tape on their mouths and unties their hands.

The family members run to Patterson and he embraces them.

> MO HONG LONG (CONT'D)
> We are in fact all in high spirits to have been invited to your last lecture, aren't we?

The lights go on above the audience.

Every single member of the crowd, from 20s to 70s, men and women of all nations, are fettered as their hands are tied behind their backs and their mouths are covered with heavy-duty tape.

Red guards from all ethnicities, but predominantly Chinese, are strategically standing in the lecture hall and holding automatic rifles.

A big screen slowly comes down from the ceiling for the audience to see.

On the screen, similar lecture halls in major countries are shown on live stream video. All have been similarly hijacked.

                    MO HONG LONG (CONT'D)
          Are we not saying that history
          is repeating itself? Hundred
          Flowers Movement ringing any
          bells, guys?
                    (beat)
          One of the backbones of the
          Cultural Revolution...
                    (beat)
          Anyone?
                    (dishearten)
          We definitely used to have a
          superior intellectual class
          back then.

Chairman Mo Hong Long picks up a detonator. He hits one of the buttons without the slightest hesitation.

The video live streams from the different countries suddenly stop, one by one, as a major explosion occurs in each of the lecture halls.

                    MO HONG LONG (CONT'D)
          We might take some of the
          blame for your simple-
          mindedness: we started long
          ago to bribe, infiltrate, and
          sabotage the West. Your big
          tech companies even sold you
          out a long time ago without
          threats or buying them off.
          Yet, there are still too many

intellectuals in your country.
Hahahahahaha!
   (beat)
Looking at all of you now
reminds me of when I was
in South America. One day,
I approached a circle of
gamblers who were betting on
roosters. After the bird's
heads were chopped off, the
rooster that ran outside the
circle first was the winner.
   (beat)
Similarly, your head was cut
off the second you sat in this
lecture hall.
   (beat)
And I bet all I've got that
you won't make it out of here
alive.
   (beat)
I'm right here, standing at
the brink of your death.
Making sure that you won't
feel a single ray of hope
while you vanish. And during
that second, I have plenty of
time to sow the seeds of a
darker shade of darkness never
witnessed before.

Chairman Mo Hong Long pushes the main button of the detonator.

EXT. CAPITOL HILL - NIGHT

A huge explosion almost destroys the whole iconic dome of Capitol Hill.

TITLE: Chinese Colony, 2025 - formerly Washington DC, U.S.A.

<u>END COLD OPEN</u>

ACT 1

EXT. WASHINGTON, D.C. STREET - DAY

A half-hearted city BUS DRIVER, in his late 50s, drives in the streets of a completely revamped Chinese totalitarian communist state.

After a few stops, his attitude starts to change: he fixes his tie and hat nicely, adjusts his posture, and changes his facial expression from indifference to earnestness, like a father preparing to greet his son after a long absence.

At the next bus stop, he enthusiastically opens the doors, but no one is there.

He waits a few seconds.

He looks around from his driver's seat perspective.

After a moment, he dares to get out of the bus, which starts a traffic jam.

He looks right and left.

He quickly gets back on the bus and heads for the next stop, his face returning to its previous wooden demeanor.

                    PASSENGER 1
                        (shouting)
                    Hey! Why did we stop for so
                    long? How can you add to the
                    burden we already go through?
                    I'll denounce you to the
                    authorities.

                    BUS DRIVER
                    Please do. Please continue to
                    deprive the world of the few
                    good people we have left. It
                    is exactly what they want.

INT. ELLIS'S BASEMENT - DAY

Tied-up, hands behind his back, and head in a closed plastic bag, ELLIS, a charming young man, mid 30s, is slowly suffocating on the floor of a cold workshop basement. He is very close to death.

INT. FRANCHISE COFFEE SHOP - DAY

A mid-20s FEMALE BARISTA absorbedly and meticulously prepares tea in a very traditional and elaborate fashion, out of sight of her coworkers.

When finished, she puts the whole thing in a regular take-out cup.

She writes ELLIS on the cup with an indelible black pen and brings it to the main counter.

She is expecting Ellis to walk in, but he doesn't show up.

> MALE BARISTA 1
> If he doesn't show up, may I have his tea?

> FEMALE BARISTA 1
> (categoric)
> No!!!!!

INT. ELLIS' BASEMENT - DAY

Ellis, still asphyxiating, is very close to death.

His cellphone, near him on the floor, with smashed screen and keyboard, starts to ring. A call from the bank.

EXT. BANK - DAY

Four big Chinese goons exit the bank and enter a large black car.

INT. SCHOOL CLASS - DAY

A classic American elementary classroom has become a communist brainwashing camp for children. Many children, around 9-10 years old and of all ethnicities, sit, intimidated and petrified with fear. They wear drab clothing, like prisoners, and a headband that monitors their behaviour and is tracked and analyzed by the flat screen computer on the teacher's desk.

An almost-robotic sounding substitute teacher drones on and on about Marxist theories.

At the back of the class, two mindful 7-years-old students, WILL (American) and LI (Chinese) are talking.

                    WILL
Is Mr. Ellis sick or what? Who the heck is that substitute anyway? He didn't even tell us his name.

                    LI
He used to have a name. The same happened to his soul. Gone. Let me check something.

Li takes some kind of measuring device from his backpack.

                LI (CONT'D)
    (looking at the indicator
      on his gadget)
It's like I thought, this guy is not human anymore.

WILL
Good thing your dad showed you how to hack these headbands. Why do I miss Mr. Ellis so much!

LI
Mr. Ellis is our oxygen mask while we are trapped in here.

WILL
It's hard to breathe when you are fed up with Marxism with Chinese characteristics.

LI
Always good for us but never applied to them.

WILL
"These teachings are the best way yet to nullify a human mind and heart."

LI
Mr. Ellis at his finest... Thanks for that balm in my existence
 (mischievous)
You know I could denounce you for saying things like that?

Li removes a handwritten list from her pocket titled *Most Wanted - WILL'S disobedience List,* showing at least 6 silly bullet points on it, and puts it on her desk.

Will picks up his own list, titled *Li's Notorious Outlaw Naughtinesses,* and puts it on his desk as well. It contains 8 amusing items about Li's behavior. They look at each other, with a serious face and then burst out laughing.

>   LI (CONT'D)
>   (looking at their lists)
>   Insulting their stupid rule
>   to report on each other
>   by bringing these to their
>   attention might be our
>   passport to forced labour
>   camps. That could increase
>   our chances of finding our
>   parents.

>   WILL
>   And if Mr. Ellis is there, we
>   could help him escape.

>   LI
>   It can't be worse than this.
>   And I've memorized Mr. Ellis's
>   best quotes, so we should be
>   fine for a while!

Will and Li both raise their hands.

INT. ELLIS'S BASEMENT - DAY

The young man is motionless, possibly far from this world.

QUICK FLASHBACK

From inside an outdoor swimming pool, a woman and man speak indistinctly to each other, their blurry silhouettes and voices are distorted.

BACK TO SCENE

Still prone on the ground, Ellis is hearing children's voices.

              CHILD 1 (O.S.)
What about his vow?

              CHILD 2 (O.S.)
He's almost out of virtue. He won't be able to take another blow without being completely destroyed, body and soul.

              CHILD 3 (O.S.)
It cannot end this way, he didn't even start to blaze his path. We cannot let him die like that.

EXT. WASHINGTON, D.C. STREET - DAY

An athletic cat walks purposefully, from one back street to the next, apparently seeking a specific destination.

It runs into some Chinese red guards chatting and laughing. It increases its pace.

Once they are aware of its presence, one of the red guards picks up his gun, raises the ante for a good bet and starts to fire at the cat, stressing the cat even more.

Leaving the alley, the cat finds itself in front of five tanks, lined up one behind another, as they were in the Tank Man video taken during the 1989 Tiananmen Square Massacre in China.

Tanks suddenly stop in front of the cat.

The cat, unmoving, seems to focus on something. Its eyes are locked on the tanks.

Tanks drive ahead at full speed.

The cat starts to run toward them.

He turns to the right side of the first tank, and uses a supernormal force to push it into an abandoned building, causing it to fall into the next street and onto a black car containing the four Chinese goons mentioned earlier. The car is totalled.

The cat slips under the second tank, and easily punches it from below. The tank is thrown a few meters into the air and crash lands on the fifth tank.

The cat then runs toward the fourth tank, jumps up and uses the gun barrel to propel it onto the third tank, causing the tanks to crash.

After this mayhem, it scoots away at an incredible speed toward a residential neighborhood.

The cat arrives on a street and runs toward a specific house. On the far side of the house, it enters using a basement window.

The four Chinese goons, shaken from their accident, are barely able to get out of their vehicle.

Another car arrives for them.

INT. ELLIS'S BASEMENT - DAY

The cat finds an inanimate body on the ground, with wrists tied behind its back and the head sealed in a plastic bag.

It approaches the plastic bag and carefully uses its teeth and claws to tear the plastic bag open and give the man some air.

It takes a few moments before Ellis starts to breathe again, which makes the cat jumpy.

The cat rushes out of the basement.

Sitting up, Ellis looks at his phone as it rings again. It's the bank still calling.

                   ELLIS
            (to the cellphone)
      You were supposed to stay dead
      this time.

Someone knocks madly on the door.

A moment later, Ellis rushes to the window where the cat entered, but there is a goon already keeping an eye on that exit. He also sees the cat in the alley, looking at him through the window, standing still as a statue.

Ellis reluctantly opens the main door.

                ELLIS (CONT'D)
     Hi! Yes I know, the bank
     meeting.

One of the four Chinese goons stands there, not at the top of his game, showing light injuries, some bleeding, and obviously exhausted. Ellis is not in the best shape either.

> Why don't we give ourselves a half hour break before we go? A first aid kit is on the wall next to the kitchen table. An expresso machine is ready to go. Please prepare coffee for your colleagues who are covering all exits while I take a quick shower.
> (beat)
> I know there is no escape from this, whatsoever.

INT. PRISON - DAY

ADRIEL, a late 40s male exuding a rare combination of finesse and grace despite wearing a prison jumpsuit, sits on a bed in an ultra-modern isolation cell, one of the few that can block supernormal abilities, that is used to induce formidable types of pain and perform intensive medical research on living subjects.

He is examining his body while holding a book.

Looking closer at himself, he sees srivatsa symbols (also called swastikas—not Hitler's symbol—the one used thousands of years ago) all over his body: knees, shoulders, palms, fingers, feet, toes, and so on.

He reads a book titled "Zhuan Falun".

Three guards chat behind bulletproof/soundproof glass, in an advanced technology surveillance office.

>   GUARD 1
>   (in Chinese, to the other
>   guards, looking at the
>   video feed from the cell)
> This book! They were supposed to have all been burned. He needs to be shot right away for having a copy of it.

>   GUARD 3
>   (in Chinese, to Guard 1)
> After you. You go shooting that freak and you will suffer the consequences for having executed a valuable prisoner.

>   GUARD 2
>   (to all guards)
> If we shoot him or even report him, how will we explain that we let him bring this book into his cell in the first

place? We will all share the
same fate.

                    GUARD 1
               (to all guards)
          They couldn't think of a worse
          job than being forced to
          watch over him? This demon is
          watching over us.

                    GUARD 3
          We don't use superstitious
          words like that, you know the
          rules.

Adriel is aware that something is
happening behind him. He turns around
and slowly walks to the back of his
cell. He can see through the wall, layer
by layer, and sees Ellis handcuffed
and sitting in a black car surrounded
by four Chinese goons, all is shown in
fluid slow motion.

Adriel turns back to the guards.

                    ADRIEL
               (friendly, in perfect
               Chinese)
          Gentlemen! Anything you
          would like to say before I
          leave this place? Any sincere
          apology might reduce the
          weight of your retribution...
          to a certain extent.

GUARD 1
(to Adriel, in English)
We won't fall for one of your tricks dem...
(look at his colleagues)
Mister!

ADRIEL
(to the guards)
Let me put it this way. Me getting out of here, along with all other prisoners in this facility, would be a cakewalk. I only want to offer you the opportunity to be the ones that let us go and earn great merit. You are welcome to join me if you want.

GUARD 1
(to Adriel)
Do you have the slightest idea of what they would do to us if --

ADRIEL
-- Actually, yes, I really do. But nothing compares with the consequences of your present hesitation. Each second you take is bringing you to deeper and deeper levels of Hell.

INT. UNKNOWN ROOM - DAY

Big and sophisticated machines print money, a lot of money. This is what most bank basements look like now.

INT. BANK MANAGER OFFICE - DAY

In a relatively small but lavish office with two glass doors, Ellis sits in front of the desk of a fat cat Chinese BANK MANAGER. Two Chinese goons are behind the bank manager, standing still and staring blankly.

>BANK MANAGER
>Let me have some privacy while we discuss your case.

With a simple touch of a small remote, the interior sides of the glass doors, that open onto the main floor of the bank, are filled with images of the scenic view from a skyscraper in Washington, DC, a city ravaged by communist infection, almost clearer than the real thing would be.

The background noise of a busy day at the bank is completely silenced by ultramodern soundproofing equipment, also activated by the remote in the bank manager's hand.

BANK MANAGER (CONT'D)
A plane could crash into that bank and we wouldn't be aware of it.

ELLIS
A crowded plane that the CCP wouldn't hesitate to hijack and crash if it would bring you another day of power.
(beat)
I bet you are using more of the technology you stole from the US. You were doing just fine harming people by launching hypersonic attacks here and there. Why be so refined all of a sudden?

BANK MANAGER
How dare you speak that way after all the Party has done for you?

ELLIS
(focuses on being calm)
Sure... Put a gun to the head of an elementary school teacher and forced him to endorse publicly that it would be in the population's best interest for all children to become state property at birth. You just needed a puppet. One solid enough to

deal with all the hate that would follow. You are right, I should be grateful.

BANK MANAGER
You forgot to mention that you have been compensated more than well, plus you had the opportunity to teach very special children.

ELLIS
The CCP is truly a huge monster with multiple heads. I rarely had a banker who knew my whole personal story in detail. That's kind of creepy.

BANK MANAGER
I guess this could be taken as a compliment to this social structure being more efficient than the previous one.

ELLIS
So efficient that the more capable the children became under my care, the more they were taken away from me by the Party.

BANK MANAGER
You assured outstanding results. Just accept being a victim of your success and

move on. You brought the children to their higher purpose.

                    ELLIS
And to thank me you offered me a typical CCP promotion: you've forced me to teach basic Marxism/Leninism/Maoism to children.

                    BANK MANAGER
It's always good to return to one's roots once in a while. We all go through this process at one point. It is only temporary.

                    ELLIS
I'll take your word for it.

                    BANK MANAGER
I understand that the disappearance of your parents --

                    ELLIS
-- Keep denying that you have anything to do with their kidnapping and probable assassination. Very efficient way to keep wounds fresh by bringing that up.

> BANK MANAGER
> I never knew anyone to stay alive more than 2 minutes when speaking so freely. You have the kind of immunity that no one can understand or even question.

> ELLIS
> Your 2 minutes feel like 2 centuries to me.

> BANK MANAGER
> Let's get back to why you are here, shall we? You have been escorted here cause of unusual bank transactions that occurred last night. Close to 4 million US dollars were transferred from your main account; but also from the credit cards that you have with us. Obscure payments have been detected.

Ellis keeps silent.

The bank manager scans through his notes on his computer.

> BANK MANAGER (CONT'D)
> After a whole night of intensive work, our investigation detected where the money was sent: to illegal

> unschooling groups, hidden
> and forbidden communism
> deprogramming centers,
> prohibited cult groups, and
> clandestine printing hideouts,
> and web creative centers not
> approved by the Party. I could
> go on.

The bank manager's phone rings. He picks it up right away, listens, and says nothing. He looks at Ellis all the while. He puts down the phone. A smile is spreading on his face.

> ELLIS
> News worth celebrating?
> Meaning bad news for the rest
> of us.

> BANK MANAGER
> Something that will shed
> some light on that case.
> Local police detectives have
> just swept your house and
> guess what they found in the
> basement...

MONTAGE - A POLICE DETECTIVE INVESTIGATES ELLIS'S BASEMENT WORKSHOP.

-- He looks closely at the vise and sees there are tie wraps next to it.

-- He discovers small pieces of glass on the workshop counter and a hammer next to them.

-- He examines a Tuck Tape roll that was cut precisely and a plastic bag with some particular holes in it.

-- A brush and powder were used to show a set of cat prints going into and out of the basement through a window.

              BANK MANAGER (CONT'D)
One hypothesis is that you have been the victim of a home invasion, left to die in your own basement as the thieves stole your credit cards. We understand the constant threats you have been under since your public statement in the media.

                    ELLIS
Seems like a pretty solid guess.

                BANK MANAGER
The problem with this hypothesis is that the transactions were done from your house and there are no signs of forced entry whatsoever.
        (beat)

The second hypothesis is that you tried to kill yourself and prior to your premeditated death, you gave everything that was yours and even what was not yours, to multiple people that the Party disapproves of.

FLASHBACK - ELLIS IS PREPARING TO COMMIT SUICIDE IN HIS BASEMENT.

-- Ellis is doing many online transactions through his bank account and using multiple credits cards.

-- He smashes his smartphone with a hammer.

-- Ellis floods his laptop with water.

-- He uses Tuck Tape to tape a plastic bag around his head.

-- He succeeds in tying his hands with a tie wrap thanks to the vise in his basement, while the plastic bag is sealed tight around his neck.

          BANK MANAGER (CONT'D)
And according to our investigation team, it wouldn't be the first time you gave money away like this. This has happened at least

4 times. You paid back your debts in a reasonable amount of time after each occurrence. You didn't raise any flags. You were more careful in the past about not leaving any traces. This time, you were kind of sloppy. If you add up these few unsuccessful suicide attempts, the bill starts to be considerable, Mr. Shortliffe. And whatever immunity you have, it won't last long when this is discovered.

ELLIS
Your hands are already full with all the killings, I only wanted to help and lighten the Party's burden.

BANK MANAGER
Killing yourself is as reprehensible as killing another citizen in this new world. Many things can be overlooked, but that is a hard stain to remove. Five failed suicide attempts, if not more, and the money you owe the Party… You don't give us many options here.

ELLIS
You have already ripped me away from my students and my parents, forced me to be your scapegoat --

BANK MANAGER
-- Ohhhh, but we recognize now our lack of judgment on how to use your full potential. We didn't foresee well enough...
(beat)
A short, but exciting, career as a disposable agent seems a better fit.

ELLIS
I'm now property of the Party like all those children whose lives I've helped to ruin. Between now and the time I'm transferred to the department in charge of the disposable agents, I'm under your full authority. I know. May I remind you they are wanting me to return in one piece. You cannot kill me. I know it will be hard for you to not cross the line. What a pity.

The bank manager closes his pen and computer screen, while cracking his fingers and neck. He seems relieved, and even excited about what is coming.

The goons are getting closer to Ellis.

> BANK MANAGER
> Remember that plane we wouldn't hear if it crashed into the bank?

Ellis doesn't make a sound.

> BANK MANAGER (CONT'D)
> It is about to happen inside this very office, without anyone from the outside knowing about it.

INT. BANK MAIN HALL - DAY

It is the busiest time of the day at the bank, as the long lineups show. NOWELL, a tall man in his 40s who has an influential vibe, enters the bank. Wearing a long coat, a hat, and holding an unorthodox state-of-the-art metallic briefcase in one hand, he waits his turn in line.

One cashier, SKYE, fighting fit male Caucasian, mid 30s, with a penetrating ability to see all details around him, including things that are about to happen, deals admirably with a customer while keeping an eye out for Nowell.

Skye is connected to a CCP SWAT team by an imperceptible communication device in his ear, that is ready to go into action. Some members of the team are on the main floor and others are at strategic vantage points.

> SKYE
> (whispering to the SWAT)
> Hold your dumbness a little bit longer.

INSERT: NOWELL SUBTLY ROLLS HIS FINGER TO SET SIX NUMBERS ON THE BRIEFCASE COMBINATION LOCK: 6-1-0-6-6-6.

Still in Nowell's hand, the briefcase opens completely. It is empty.

He seems amused by the fact that his briefcase opened as it was an accident, and he closes it immediately.

After seeing the inside of Nowell's briefcase, Skye looks relieved.

Nowell continues to stand in line and starts staring at his watch without blinking.

Skye receives an alert from his computer indicating that the printer room in the bank basement has a problem.

INT. BANK BASEMENT - DAY

The money printing machines under the bank have stopped working. They are smoking, and sparks and small fires are visible.

INT. BANK MAIN HALL - DAY

> SWAT TEAM LEADER (O.S.)
> (in Chinese)
> We have reason to believe that there are some problems downstairs, sir. The printers are not responding anymore. We are going in.

> SKYE
> (in Chinese)
> Negative. Target is almost acquired. That is still the primary objective. Whatever happens downstairs can wait. If any member of your team blows this you will all have to attend my masterclass on professionalism.

While keeping one eye on his watch, Nowell rolls the numbers on the locks and discreetly opens his briefcase again but only a few centimeters.

He waits 10 seconds and closes it by changing two numbers on the lock.

Skye talks to a colleague to arrange for him to be replaced for a while.

Nowell intercepts one of Skye's glimpses at him. He decides to leave the line and slowly walks toward the nearest exit.

Skye picks up his pace and is now walking at a good trot towards Nowell.

Skye suddenly stops when he sees some red laser light dots on the bodies of some of the clients waiting in line on the main floor. The light was an accident caused by a distracted sniper SWAT member.

When one of the clients notices a red dot, mass hysteria breaks out. Civilians run everywhere looking for a place to hide.

    SKYE (CONT'D)
  (to SWAT team, in English)
OK, early bird price to my masterclass for all of you.
  (speaking to the
  security system with his
  communication device)
Lock down the bank's main doors. Shut down video cameras and audio feeds. Only allow incoming communication.
  (to the cashiers)
Evacuate the civilians by the back door.

Skye grabs a handgun from the back waistband of his pants, and loads a cartridge of unconventionally sharp bullets.

With one clean and precise shot he shoots the sniper who made the mistake.

Cashiers show the civilians the way out of the bank.

The bank main doors lock electronically as indicated on a computer screen.

Swarming in from all corners of the bank, SWAT members reveal themselves, all are aiming their guns at Skye.

As promised, Skye astoundingly kills all members of the tactical team, one after another, emptying charger after charger of armor-piercing bullets.

Some aim at the innocents running toward the main door; but Skye doesn't allow them to shoot. He takes down all those who try.

Nowell, with his case in one hand, draws a gun with the other.

Members of the SWAT team encircle him, pointing their automatic weapons at him.

INT. BANK BASEMENT - DAY

Some of the members of the CCP SWAT team try to reduce the damage from the fire engulfing the printers and the money piles using extinguishers. Most extinguishers fizzle out in a few seconds because they are out dated. Some of the team members use fire blankets, as others become human torches.

INT. BANK MAIN HALL - DAY

Nowell has his hands raised in the air and prepares to put his handgun on the floor.

Skye makes sure to eliminate all threats around Nowell while moving closer to him.

Nowell and Skye are the last people standing. Nowell points his gun at Skye.

                    NOWELL
  I thought you were --

                    SKYE
  -- The bad guy?
      (reloading his gun with
      regular bullets and aiming
      at Nowell)
  Kind of. Well, it is hard to
  tell even for me.
      (to his communication
      device, in Chinese)

>   Please don't send any backup.
>   I've got the situation under
>   control. Skye out.

Skye removes his communication device from his ear and smashes it on the floor with his foot.

EXT. EUROPEAN RESTAURANT - DAY

On the terrace of a sunny European style restaurant in Washington D.C., Adriel, the only client in the middle of the afternoon, wears sunglasses and a smile. He asks the truly devoted WAITRESS for the menu.

>   ADRIEL
>   May I have the menu please?

>   WAITRESS
>   Again? That's the fourth time.

>   ADRIEL
>   You miss a lot of meals when
>   you're in a re-education camp.
>   Guards suggested this place to
>   reconnect with the world when
>   you haven't eaten well for a
>   long time.

>   WAITRESS
>   Some of my family members are
>   in one of those places.

ADRIEL
I'm sincerely sorry to hear that.

WAITRESS
This will sound odd, but it is the first time I can feel genuine compassion from the words that people say over and over.

ADRIEL
After having been in many of these detention centers, each time I get out, I find fewer differences with the outside world.

WAITRESS
Somehow you left the place with a pair of sunglasses.

ADRIEL
One of the guards offered them to me.

WAITRESS
That sounds highly improbable.

ADRIEL
The more you talk to me, the more far-fetched things will get.

                    WAITRESS
Like your smile?

                    ADRIEL
I have a fake smile?

                    WAITRESS
I have been puzzled since you
arrived. Why does someone
smile that much?

                    ADRIEL
                 (genuine)
Was it banned while I was
away?

                    WAITRESS
Hahahaha! We are getting close
to that, but not yet. It is
just... You've been here for
few hours now and your smile
hasn't faded one bit.

                    ADRIEL
Even though apparently there
is not a single reason to
smile, remember that when we
do it is only for "apparent"
reasons. In fact, I must
admit that I've had quite an
interesting time --

                    WAITRESS
-- You mean... With this cat.

The cat previously seen in the basement is sitting on the chair right in front of Adriel.

ADRIEL
Well... This is not a --

WAITRESS
-- Do you have some kind gift to communicate with animals?

ADRIEL
Yes. I have a kind of gift to talk with...
(beat)
I should get going as you are about to get really busy here. How many seats do you have in this place?

WAITRESS
Well, around 50 seats. But it won't be busy before, let's say, five...

ADRIEL
We would love to stay, but if we do, you won't have enough seats available.

A crowd of people, obviously disoriented and wearing ragged clothing provided by a detention center, arrives at the restaurant entrance.

                    ADRIEL (CONT'D)
          The guards where I was
          prisoner are buying. Not just
          for what I got but for all
          these people. Here they are!

Guards seen previously are guiding the
group.

                    ADRIEL (CONT'D)
          Time to call your husband.

                    WAITRESS
               (stammering)
          Time to what?

                    ADRIEL
               (pointing with his finger)
          Aren't they your step-parents?

INT. BANK MAIN HALL - DAY

Bodies of the CCP SWAT team litter the
floor like dead flies—all are immobile.

Skye and Nowell point guns at each
other.

The office where Ellis and the bank
manager and his goons are, is located
between the two armed men.

Suddenly, the glass doors explode into
thousands of pieces as Ellis is thrown
through them and lands on the ground,

in the middle of Nowell and Skye's stand-off.

Skye draws a second gun from his waistband aiming it in the direction of Ellis, the bank manager and the goons, who are obviously worse for wear, while still aiming a gun at Nowell.

> SKYE
> Leave by the emergency back exit, now!

The bank manager and goons obey and immediately shuffle out.

The bodies of two dead SWAT members lie between Nowell and Skye each holding loaded handguns that Ellis can easily grasp.

He rolls over, picks up both guns and points them at Nowell and Skye while clumsily getting to his feet.

> ELLIS
> (to both Nowell and Skye)
> What a bizarre feeling to be thrown through a skyscraper window but experience such a short fall before hitting the ground.
> (looking at Skye, lowers the gun aimed at Skye)
> Colonel Wakefield?

                    SKYE
          You are mistaken. You must
          have been confused by your...
          strange fall.

                    ELLIS
          C'mon Colonel! Was your head
          injured during the invasion or
          what...
               (beat)
          Don't tell me you have also
          taken the black pill?

Ellis aims his gun back at Skye.

                    NOWELL
               (stepping slowly away)
          Maybe I'll let you both focus
          on your unexpected reunion...

                    SKYE
               (to Nowell)
          You're not going anywhere. And
          drop the good guy act for a
          second! Whatever you came here
          for, you only have the option
          of eliminating both of us to
          maintain your cover. That's
          how even heroes act in times
          like these.

                    NOWELL
               (to Ellis)
          The way he has wiped out this
          entire SWAT team...

(beat)
I can say that the colonel you once knew is gone.

SKYE
(to both)
You would be dead, and many other innocents too, if I hadn't intervened. I was instructed to eliminate them if they messed up again. Make space for new recruits, trained using Americans standards instead of their shitty CCP ones.
(beat)
They cannot find capable American soldiers to train their worldwide army as fast as they would like. Oh, and they will kill me if this mission fails or if that team fails in any way. Being picky when choosing your employer is a luxury from the past.

Nowell and Ellis look at him, both are quiet for a micro-second.

ELLIS
Maybe I should have played dead while you completed your conversation. But I'm not very good at it.

SKYE
Bad at what?

ELLIS
Playing dead.

NOWELL
What is that supposed to mean?

ELLIS
Never mind.

NOWELL
We are kind of short on rationality and reason here. Maybe you act as a mediator for the greater good?

SKYE
The greater good has been on backorder for a while I'm afraid.
(to Ellis)
As crazy as it sounds, the safest place you can be now is here. But keep aiming at both of us, just in case. You never know how things will unfold.

SKYE (CONT'D)
(to Nowell, looking at his briefcase)
What's the story with your case? Something tells me that

it is too fancy and too small for robbing a bank.

                    NOWELL
I'm here...
    (beat)
To kill the money.

                    SKYE
Say what—use a bit more polished English?

                    NOWELL
To stop the Chinese communists from debauching the currency.

                    ELLIS
"Debauching the currency"?

                    NOWELL
One of the first things they did after the insurrection was destroy capitalism once and for all.

                    SKYE
    (laughing)
Are you that naive? It was Lenin's but he never succeeded in implementing it. The CCP has learned to use and master capitalism to --

                    ELLIS
          -- To add fuel to the
          gruesomeness of its crimes.

                    NOWELL
          Anyway, they just want
          to unsettle the previous
          world, causing endless
          hyperinflation, just another
          way to squeeze us by the
          balls, but even more tightly
          this time. They have outfitted
          banks with vast underground
          rooms to print money, day and
          night, all around the globe.

                    SKYE
          How did you hack the bank's
          printers?

                    NOWELL
          Not hacked. Crushed them.
          Nano-robotics.

MONTAGE/FLASHBACK - NANOBOTS HAVE THE
MISSION OF DESTROYING THE MONEY PRINTERS
AND BURNING PILES OF PAPER BILLS.

-- Around 10 nanobots were activated
when Nowell first opened his briefcase
and released them.

-- Once on the floor, they went to the
money printing room they located using
an internal GPS.

-- A few nanobots destroyed the security cameras and corrupted the sprinkler system by freezing them.

-- They entered different parts of the printers and sabotaged them using lasers.

-- Some nanobots scanned the room with a green light and set fire to the newlt printed money piled on the floor.

-- The nanobots came back to the briefcase when Nowell opened it the second time.

>   NOWELL (CONT'D)
>   (to Skye)
>   I sense a lack of eagerness to
>   bring this technology back to
>   the CCP.

>   ELLIS
>   (to Skye)
>   This is your way out, right?
>   Your bargaining chip?

>   SKYE
>   They cannot be allowed to have
>   this in their hands. Trust
>   me. Being on the inside, I've
>   seen how they manufacture
>   nightmares. Adding even that
>   small toy to their tyrannical

imperium is something you would do anything to prevent.

                    ELLIS
Wait. What if...
     (to Nowell)
What if you are giving them exactly what they want?

                    SKYE
What's your point?

                    ELLIS
What if they are mass producing money on the surface, but meanwhile, planning something... worse. Think like the CCP. Further twist your most twisted thoughts.

                    SKYE
     (to Nowell)
They could use you and the people with you to get rid of the printers and money for them. A bait. Then frame all of it on you. They are making sure that the resistance focuses its attention elsewhere while they are planning something more sinister all the while...

ELLIS
(thinking)
What would be better than overprinting money?

SKYE
(thinking)
A cashless society. The perfect storm for tracking any transaction, and knowing their citizen's every move. Eradicate privacy. Push for ultimate control.

NOWELL
And their schemes always imply turning on each other in the process.

ELLIS
(to Nowell)
What you did today was probably not done just locally, but on a global scale, right?

NOWELL
Yes.

ELLIS
You need to abort this operation now.

                    SKYE
          It's too late. Anyone involved
          is probably already dead. I
          was assigned to this location.

INT. MULTIPLE BANKS ALL AROUND THE WORLD
- EARLIER

A few of Nowell's men complete the
destruction of the printing rooms and
extra money hideouts in different bank
basements using the nanobot technology.

Their escapes all end the same way: they
are intercepted and shot by CCP agents.

Each CCP agent picks-up the special
cases used by their victims.

BACK TO PRESENT

                    SKYE
             (screaming)
          It means you have made them
          one step more invincible.

                    NOWELL
          They may have wiped out all of
          my team, but the technology
          is safe. If each person is not
          reporting every 10 minutes to
          the base, a self-destruction
          device automatically
          activates.

INT. MULTIPLE BANKS ALL AROUND THE WORLD - EARLIER

Each CCP agent is carring a special case containing the nanobot technology. After a moment, the cases explode, killing or severely injuring the holders.

BACK TO PRESENT

          SKYE (V.O.)
Destroying this technology won't be enough. They will find anyone linked to this and extract the technology from their brain if they need to, even if they are dead. I've seen them recover information in ways you wouldn't believe exist.
They will send me or other agents to find you and any survivors from your team.
    (beat)
But you can die now by my hand, I'll make sure they never find your body. Leaving them no chance. Or...
    (beat)
You die later in their torture chambers, brain-dead from their attempts to extract your secrets, and being haunted until your last breath by the regret of not taking my offer.

You don't want them to be more
unstoppable than they are.

                    NOWELL
Why don't you give it a shot?

                    ELLIS
          (to Skye, shouting)
No!

Skye pulls the trigger, but instead of
firing a bullet, the gun dismantles
itself piece by piece. He shoots the
second gun and the same thing happens.

                    ELLIS (CONT'D)
What happened?

FLASHBACK: In the bank hall, a few
nanobots go back into Nowell's briefcase
while others go inside Skye's guns and
destroy them slowly from the inside.

BACK TO PRESENT

Ellis looks at his guns and realizes he
has the balance of power because they
weren't damaged by Nowell's nanobots.

A few meters away, a surviving guard
aims at Nowell and shoots him in the
leg.

Ellis shoots at the guard's gun and the
smoke grenade on his belt, which creates

a massive cloud in that part of the bank.

Skye succeeds in picking up an automatic weapon from one of the dead SWAT team members on the floor and points it at Nowell.

Nowell is about to shoot Skye.

Ellis fires at Skye and Nowell: one bullet hits Skye's shoulder, bringing him down and causing him to lose his weapon. The second hits Nowell's gun.

Beeping starts emanating from the briefcase, still in Nowell's hand.

          ELLIS (CONT'D)
      (to Nowell)
  What is that?

            NOWELL
  I need to let the base know that I'm still in possession of the nanobots.

            ELLIS
  You aren't. Toss it over. We are all quite aware of what follows.

Nowell throws the case about ten meters behind him, where there is no one. The signal beeps faster and faster until the briefcase detonates.

> **NOWELL**
> They are all gone. The others will gradually, automatically self-destruct as well.

Ellis looks at a dead SWAT team member on the floor.

> **ELLIS**
> (to Nowell)
> Put his gear on and take one of these bodies with you. It will help you to sneak out of here and blend in.

> **SKYE**
> What about me?

An earpiece on the floor squawks a message. Ellis puts it in his ear.

Nowell puts his ear next to the head of the dead SWAT person he carries.

> **EARPIECE**
> (semi-audible)
> I repeat. Disposable agent package ready to be acquired at the bank under the name of Mister Ellis Shortliffe. This is now the main objective.

Locating Nowell is now a secondary objective.

> NOWELL
> Outside of tearing apart all families on the planet, what have you done to be more valuable than this piece of technology?

> ELLIS
> I'm still trying to figure that out.

> NOWELL
> Still having doubts about being here by chance?

> ELLIS
> I'm not at the stage of asking myself that kind of question.

Skye takes another gun from a dead SWAT man lying on the floor. Ellis, almost without looking, shoots Skye again in his other shoulder, making him drop his newly acquired gun.

> SKYE
> (to Ellis)
> Can you stop shooting at me... with your non-lethal techniques?

ELLIS
You show me them. They are on you.

NOWELL
(to Ellis)
Maybe he is right.
(beat)
We are also in possession of several other technologies...

ELLIS
Just when we got some closure...

SKYE
Finally! Coming to his senses.

Ellis is paralyzed by confusion.

NOWELL
Among these technologies that we have acquired... We have the capacity to engineer memory.

ELLIS
You mean...

NOWELL
We can implant or erase memory.

                    ELLIS
          Has it been tested? Does it
          really work?

                    NOWELL
          Yes. It's ready to use if
          necessary.

                    ELLIS
          I will not call the shots
          from now on. You decide to
          wash out any trace of these
          technologies from your brain
          and anyone you care about or
          make sure you use them against
          Goliath. The only stand I take
          is to not kill you. I hope
          this will bring some blessings
          to all of us in the long run.

                    NOWELL
          You are a religious man. I
          knew it.

                    ELLIS
          I guess I needed to figure
          that out too. On my "to-do
          list."

Nowell puts a wounded SWAT team member over his shoulder and escapes through the back of the bank. Ellis runs to Skye.

                    SKYE
          By not killing him and letting
          him go, you have killed me,
          yourself, and all of us.

                    ELLIS
          You've received some updates.
               (beat)
          You are about to complete your
          mission.

Ellis puts his handgun in Skye's hand.

EXT. X BANK - DAY

Skye opens the main doors while aiming a handgun at Ellis's head. CCP troops harshly pick Ellis up while paramedics take care of Skye. Some military and police personnel praise him.

                    SKYE
               (subtly to Ellis)
          If this world becomes a
          slightly more horrible place
          after these choices of yours,
          I will personally hold you
          responsible!

ACT 2

INT. MILITARY HOSPITAL FACILITY - DAY

Ellis, in a basic hospital gown, waits in a doctor's examination room. His face shows that he was beaten weeks ago. Every injury on his face has almost healed. He seems more resilient, level-headed, and somehow stronger than he was previously.

MONTAGE/FLASHBACK: Ellis - with no signs of injury - is studied as a lab rat.

-- He walks on a treadmill that suddenly goes backward, which puzzles Ellis.

-- A doctor prepares to give Ellis a shot, but the needle bends instead of piercing his arm.

-- Ellis goes through some precision shooting tests. He shoots different targets, in different sets, and is quite accurate sometimes impressively so.

-- He runs on the treadmill, backward.

-- A doctor takes some blood samples from Ellis and puts them in a refrigerator.

-- Ellis is in a hand-to-hand combat test, where he is beaten-up because his basic skills are useless against the ruthless adversaries.

-- Opening the blood storage refrigerator, a doctor picks out a bag of Ellis's blood and transfuses it into him.

-- He goes through different writing tests, his face swollen from the previous fight training. A few drops of his blood drip on one of the documents that he is filling out. More blood droplets splatter onto most of the documents on the table.

-- Many doctors are performing surgery around an operating table.

-- There is an ice bag on one of his ears that gets in the way while undergoing some auditory tests.

-- A doctor tries a second time to give Ellis a shot but this time, the liquid squirts out of the syringe.

-- Behind an eye testing machine, tears roll down one of Ellis' cheeks.

-- He endures a series of interviews with different groups of people in different settings. He speaks slowly because his injured jaw is painful.

-- Round 2 in a hand-to-hand combat test. He manages some impressive hits in an ocean of average moves. He gets beaten up again.

DR RETH, a slightly chubby Uyghur physician in his 60s who carries the burden of unhealed grief, enters the examination room and sits at his desk.

                    ELLIS
I won't have anything against you if you cut right to the chase and do whatever you need to do as quickly as possible. I wouldn't mind if you take this opportunity to break a world record for completing a consultation.

                    DR RETH
You wouldn't believe how devastating it is to be impatient on the molecular plane.

                    ELLIS
Sure, Dr Emoto.

                    DR RETH
My name is Dr Reth.

ELLIS
I'll stick with Dr Emoto for now.

Dr Reth performs a regular medical check-up on Ellis: he examines his eyes, ears, blood pressure, all while talking with him.

ELLIS (CONT'D)
As my face and my cells seem to have no secrets from you, I'll let them do the talking.

DR RETH
They've told me quite a lot already. Still need to do what regular doctors do though... so you feel reassured.

ELLIS
Wait. Are you not a real doctor?

DR RETH
You could say I'm closer to what used to be an ancient Chinese medicine doctor.

ELLIS
What is that supposed to mean? Nonsense is starting to seriously pile up.

DR RETH
Are you familiar with the term MK Ultra or Project Monarch?

ELLIS
Yes. I've heard they program and control people to do anything: assassination, sex slavery, or other things. Urban legend says most teachers, from kindergarten to university, are under its influence.

DR RETH
The CCP is using it without restraint since they arrived in the US. With communism messing up humankind since it first came into being, it has progressively weakened human thinking, making this the perfect time for mass use. 9/10 of the Disposable Agents are under the control of MK Ultra. Collapsing your psychological state, falling into sarcasm and irony as you tend to do, they will just press a button and you will be gone. Blacked-pilled. You become... them. Instantly. From head to toe. Cultivating enthusiasm is the only way my friend.

ELLIS
I might review a few of my defense mechanisms then.

DR RETH
Upgrading your literal defense system would be a good idea as well.
(beat)
The invasion happened so quickly. The training you received during the short conscription was flagrantly insufficient for what you are about to experience. But don't worry, I'll make sure they call you a late bloomer in hand-to-hand combat.

ELLIS
(joking)
You'll train me? Hahahaha!

DR RETH
Hahahahha! No. Hahahahaha!
(beat)
I'd create a foe so formidable that even I would have a hard time stopping it.

ELLIS
Hahahaha! That good, huh?
(beat)
Let's suppose for one second that what you say is true,

maybe that would help to free us all from the CCP.

> DR RETH

I seriously doubt that. You would hastily develop a taste for killing. The CCP world view would now make more sense to you as they would provide plenty of opportunities for you to get your daily fix. This doesn't include the fact that you could become hungry for power. The higher your kill count, the more you rise to the top. The environment they created is the perfect incubator for evil to transcend.

> ELLIS

I was not expecting this diagnostic today. I'd like to say I'm shocked, but I haven't felt that way for quite a while.

> DR RETH

I've read that your shooting skills are impressive, probably past life related, but we also have to give some credit to your instructor.

FLASHBACK: Under heavy rain at night, Ellis, and other men, train with different firearms under the orders of Colonel Wakefield, first name Skye.

                    ELLIS
               (laughing)
I still have a hard time picturing you as a physician. What's your story?

                    DR RETH
I became unfit for duty at a certain point in my life, so they forced me to enter their medical program.

                    ELLIS
Unfit for duty?

                    DR RETH
Some of us were targeted to become expendable agents at a very young age.

                    ELLIS
Are Expendable Agents --

                    DR RETH
-- That's what they called it in the past. CCP players were stealing babies in different areas that were already under persecution in China before the US insurrection, such as

the Xinjiang part of China,
where I come from.
    (beat)
We were assigned to do the
dirtiest of the dirtiest jobs
for the CCP. One day, I was
stroked by...
    (beat)
As crazy as it sounds, I am
starting to see everything at
a microcosmic level due to the
sudden activation of my pineal
gland.

              ELLIS
Your third eye?

              DR RETH
Celestial Eye is a more
accurate way to describe it.
    (beat)
I started to see the carnage
I was perpetrating from an
endless, enhanced perspective.
Then, my killer instinct
instantly dried up, and I
was unable to perpetrate
any more bloodshed. Young,
under threat, and after
conditioning, most of us
learned to become cold-
hearted murderers. But when
you see everything under
the microscope of the cosmic
truth, you cannot act against

any sentient being for any reason. So many cosmic laws have become clear to me.

                    ELLIS
          Do they know? About... this?

Ellis points at the location of the third eye on his forehead.

                    DR RETH
          No. But at first, I was a
          fascinating lunatic for them
          to study. They spent time
          carefully observing how I
          became overly and obsessively
          caring about the living, and
          even the non-living. They
          understood that it was in
          their best interest to keep me
          on their side. Mostly to cover
          their own asses.

                    ELLIS
          So your job description
          includes nothing less than
          keeping these fiends alive?

                    DR RETH
          That is one way to put it. And
          the asses of some disposable
          agents.

ELLIS
Sharing all these things with me can't be good for your social credit. I assume that no one is listening, right?

DR RETH
Actually, they are.
  (beat)
They hear my voice. And yours. But everything we say is not what they hear.

ELLIS
Sorry, you've lost me.
  (beat)
In fact, I've been lost since you said you were not Dr Emoto.

DR RETH
Remember the Deepfake program? Putting anyone's face on anyone's body by computer? The CCP framed most of their rivals that way. It is even easier to do using speech to defame. Constructing simple and coherent sentences that don't trigger their sensors is nothing.

ELLIS
Anything to protect doctor/patient confidentiality, fancy that.

Someone knocks loudly on the door. Dr Reth opens it.

A CCP military person hands him a yellow envelope.

He closes the door, sits back, and puts the envelope on his desk without opening it.

ELLIS (CONT'D)
I must confess, I don't feel reassured by knowing that you are not that unmerciful assassin anymore but are extremely skilled at cherishing and extending life itself...

DR RETH
That's your worst nightmare, isn't it? Hahahaha!

Dr Reth stands up, stretches a bit and picks up the yellow envelope.

DR RETH (CONT'D)
Let's stretch those weak legs of yours, shall we?

                    ELLIS
          Did they ask for this?

INT. MILITARY HOSPITAL HALLWAY - DAY

Dr Reth walks with Ellis.

He holds the yellow envelope in his hands.

Some CCP army members move nearer the wall, afraid of Dr Reth.

                    ELLIS
          Can you... prescribe anything
          close to permanent peace to
          the disposable agents?

                    DR RETH
          Even doctors cannot prescribe
          any painkillers whatsoever.
          We are not even using them
          in the hospital anymore. They
          have been forbidden since the
          insurrection. And don't turn to
          the black market because the
          CCP controls that as well. They
          have engineered pain enhancers
          identical to painkillers to
          trick the ones that want to
          lighten up the ride.
               (beat)
          Have you heard about the
          illegal app that displays all

forms of true art from the
past?

ELLIS
I cannot live without it.

DR RETH
Well it is probably one of the
very few forms of relief out
there. Definitely better that
the CCP psychological warfare
of sending pictures and videos
of people being tortured to
everyone's smartphone.
(beat)
Oh! Here's our stop.

Dr Reth stops at a door labelled MORGUE.

INT. MORGUE - DAY

Innumerable body bags lie on tables.
Ellis and Dr Reth walk between them.

ELLIS
Lovely pit stop. Got anything
to eat around here?

DR RETH
I've talked to you about my
transition from killer to
doctor, right? Your instructor
was forced to take the
opposite path.

ELLIS
I recently got a glimpse of that.

DR RETH
He was an honorable doctor once, but that was a long time ago. His grandfather was an icon in the military, from whom he learned in his youth the things he taught you and many others. But the CCP got him during his second year of medical practice as he was becoming a promising surgeon. And, they found a way to crush him.

ELLIS
These bodies...

DR RETH
This is Skye's doing. Not the bodies you previously saw at the bank. This is just a sample of his everyday life.

ELLIS
It cannot be... He can't be the only one responsible for this.

DR RETH
Your cells showed me that not only Skye and I were sent on a killer trajectory... but you

went down that road as well. Continuously trying to put the same person in one of these bags...

INT. X-RAY ROOM - DAY

Ellis and Dr Reth examine an empty X-Ray illuminator.

> ELLIS
> Is something supposed to appear or are we just burning our retinas looking at this light?

> DR RETH
> I just waited a second to make a better impression. Here we go!

Dr Reth removes a few CT scans of a brain from the yellow envelope he still carried and places them on the illuminator.

> DR RETH (CONT'D)
> One communist principle is to undervalue human life. No Gods. No afterlife. No nothing. Not even consequences if you take your own life.

Dr Reth points to at least 5 different spots on the CT scans.

DR RETH (CONT'D)
Even on a superficial plane, we can see here every time you tried to kill yourself, it left marks on your brain.
(beat)
You have no idea what it represents at the molecular level, do you?

ELLIS
(shamefully)
No...

DR RETH
Ancient Chinese medicine considered the human body to be a small universe. If your body is a small universe, and you succeed in shutting it down, can you start to imagine the death sentences of countless beings in your cosmos? There is no human term to explain such mass extinction.

ELLIS
(stunned)
There are probably no human words in defense of this, I suppose...

DR RETH
Have you heard how the CCP usually deals with suicidal people?

ELLIS
Torture them by confining them in a morgue refrigerator or bury them for hours. Another way I heard of is letting them bleed out for hours and then bringing them back to life just before they die. That kind of reckoning. I heard that the worst of all is being recruited as a disposable agent.

DR RETH
Sadly, there is no shortcut to finding permanent peace. Or --

ELLIS
-- Or what...?

DR RETH
Well you know. We could say there is a last chance for real peace.

ELLIS
I can't do it.

DR RETH
Think about it. You wouldn't need to see any doctors anymore.

ELLIS
It couldn't hurt. Kind of funny to hear this suggestion from a "doctor." Trying to put yourself out of business?

DR RETH
Why do you think I'm less and less busy?

ELLIS
So you suggest that I add risk and danger to an already precarious line of work?

DR RETH
No loss no gain.

ELLIS
I'm considering passing by the MK Ultra Brainwash Center right after this.

DR RETH
Ohhh...

ELLIS
I'm kidding.

> DR RETH
> Just give Falun Dafa another try and you will see.

> ELLIS
> My parents gave me the same advice before they were abducted by the Party. But wait, another try? How do you --

> DR RETH
> -- I can see how you have benefitted from it...

> ELLIS
> But I practiced the exercises only a couple of times... Can my cells not shush themselves once in a while?

Dr Reth picks up a pad and fills out a prescription for Ellis. He tears the slip off and gives it to him.

> DR RETH
> You would need to meet a therapist and a nutritionist.

> ELLIS
> Do I really need to --

> DR RETH
> -- Don't put emphasis on their occupations. These are among

                    the last decent human beings
                    left... Just consider it a
                    treat.

Someone is knocking at the door.

                    DR RETH (CONT'D)
                    Time's up. They will give you
                    a quick break, a night off.
                    Try to enjoy it as much as you
                    can.

Dr Reth seems to believe half of what he said. He tries to hide the worry that shows on his face.

EXT. BAR - SUNSET

In a scenic resort-like view, where nothing bad could happen, Ellis waits at an outside bar wearing relaxed and stylish clothing. A burnt out BARMAN comes close to Ellis.

                    BARMAN
                    What will it be sir? It's on
                    the house.

                    ELLIS
                (peaceful)
                    Is that so?
                (beat)
                    Asking for something strong
                    is useless as the reality is
                    always something stronger. To

>   make a real contrast, please
>   serve me something... Discreet.
>   Settling.
>   Delicate.

The barman finds a really fancy bottle and serves a nice glass of water to Ellis.

>   BARMAN
>   A purist, with all my respect.
>   Here's water for you, Sir.

>   ELLIS
>   Thanks a lot.

He savors each sip.

A WOMAN, a femme fatale who convincingly plays the innocence card, approaches the bar.

>   WOMAN
>   (to the barman)
>   I'll have the same as the
>   gentleman here.

The barman opens a different fancy bottle and serves some water to the unidentified woman.

>   WOMAN (CONT'D)
>   (to Ellis)
>   How's your disposable agent
>   training?

                    ELLIS
               (focused)
          Please, don't make trouble
          now. You can only drink
          something like this with quiet
          reverence.

Ellis slowly takes a sip.

                    ELLIS (CONT'D)
          For this precise moment, I
          don't care if you are on the
          opposite team lusting for
          power, another disposable
          agent, or if you are among the
          millions of people threatened
          and made to act against their
          will. Whoever you are, in this
          instant, I'm fine with it and
          won't interfere. For our sakes,
          let's cherish this.

                    WOMAN
          I'm not here for power. I'm
          certainly not a disposable
          agent and neither have I been
          threatened with anything...

                    ELLIS
          How can it be...

                    WOMAN
          I don't...remember... anything.

Ellis opens one eye and glimpses at her arm. He sees many puncture marks on her forearms.

            ELLIS
    Do you recall whether they
    injected you at all?

            WOMAN
    Not precisely... but that could
    explain all these holes and
    the pain in my arms.

            ELLIS
    You must have been subjected
    to experimental drugs that
    just scattered your whole
    being, if you survive them.
    At least you are alive. Or
    could we call it bad luck?
    You might as well have been
    through electroshock or sleep
    deprivation, there are a
    myriad of ways to explain your
    memory loss.
        (beat)
    But in your case, I bet you
    are faking it.

The woman draws a gun from her back. A green light lights up on the barrel followed by a clicking sound.

Ellis reenters a tranquil state, drinks a last sip, and puts his glass on the bar with rare gentleness.

He starts to try to disarm her but as their skills are both half-baked, it looks more like they are dancing.

Eventually, during the dance, he succeeds in grabbing her gun.

A red light appears, and a locking mechanism clicks, making the gun unusable for Ellis.

The dance continues until Ellis gets her gun again, his hand on her hand, his finger on her finger, both on the trigger. The green light comes back on and the gun barrel points at the woman's head.

In the periphery, Ellis senses that the barman is aiming a gun at him.

The barman also has this weird gun that seems to only unlock when held by its owner.

> ELLIS (CONT'D)
> (to the barman)
> Put your gun down! She played me. And you. Give me your handkerchief.

The barman gives it to Ellis and he
rubs off the fake needle marks on her
forearms.

>   ELLIS (CONT'D)
>   (to the barman)
>   Yours, though, are real...

Ellis falls to the ground.

His arms extended, the barman shows
the real needle marks that expose the
terrible treatment he was subjected to.

The woman takes control of the
situation.

>   WOMAN
>   (to Ellis)
>   Just sorting out one thing...
>   (beat)
>   Will you fight for your life
>   in the deeper states of
>   consciousness or will you just
>   continually tune out like you
>   do on the surface?

Ellis is floored by the drug that was in
his water, but somehow finds the energy
to get up and hang on to a bar stool.

>   WOMAN (CONT'D)
>   Impossible.

The woman's eyes are locked onto Ellis', as she wants him to fall again. She manages to trip him by kicking the bar seat Ellis is holding. Ellis falls again, and stays down this time.

> WOMAN (CONT'D)
> That's more like it.

INT. TUNNEL - UNKNOWN

Ellis wakes up lying on a cold and dark metallic floor. Slowly standing up, he looks around: he is in a huge metallic tunnel with long curved grooves carved in the sides, as if inside the barrel of a gun.

He notices a light in front of him... The light at the end of the tunnel.

> ELLIS (V.O.)
> (to himself)
> Can it be?
> (beat)
> Everything comes to you when you stop looking for it as they say. Finally.

The more Ellis goes towards the light, the more it recedes. The more he backs up, the more the light advances toward him.

                    ELLIS (V.O.)
          Nice! Never heard of that
          version of the light at the
          end of the tunnel.

Ellis starts to walk backward while
still facing the light.

From the back of the tunnel, he hears an
explosion that sounds louder and louder.

Ellis considers running toward the
light. After a few seconds, he decides
to turn around completely, and run
toward the unbearable sound, which will
make the light advance more quickly.

The sound of the explosion becomes
louder and louder.

Ellis suddenly sees a colossal bullet
coming toward him, with a trail of fire
behind it. He is getting closer to the
light.

Confident, he continues running until
the bullet and light become one with
Ellis.

EXT. MILITARY COMPLEX - LATER

From Ellis' perspective, he sees eyes
opening and closing, as Dr Reth pushes
him on a gurney.

DR RETH
I had to green light that
extra test they insisted on
performing on you. It is the
first time they required this.
Whatever happened while you
passed out, you have blown
them away. I have never seen
them that nervous.
   (beat)
Don't worry, what you drank was
only Chinese medicinal herbs.
My original dosage was pretty
concentrated. The hardest
thing was to create a tasteless
version of it. Hope you didn't
have too much of a bad trip.
Not only will you be functional
in no time, but it will remove
a lot of crap they injected
into you before and will alter
their tracers. I only agreed
to go along with the procedure
because it gave us the
opportunity to keep you under
observation—giving you more
time. You will use it to meet
her before it is too late...

EXT. MILITARY MEDICAL FACILITY CHECK
POINT - NIGHT

Dr Reth drives his car to leave the
premises.

An overzealous GUARD (1) knocks hard on the driver's window of Dr Reth's car.

> GUARD 1
> (in Chinese)
> Inspection. Open the back doors.

Dr Reth starts to feel anxious.

The loutish guard carefully inspects the back of the car.

In the checkpoint booth, another GUARD (2) eats instant noodles.

Raising his eyes, Guard 2 sees Dr Reth and his colleague.

He quickly abandons his noodles, which fall all over the floor.

Guard 2 runs to the car.

> GUARD 1 (CONT'D)
> (in Chinese, to Dr Reth)
> Open the trunk. Now!

Dr Reth puts his finger on the trunk button. Right before he activates the opening of the trunk, Guard 2 from the security booth grabs Guard 1 and pushes him onto the wall of the booth.

> GUARD 2
> (in Chinese, quietly)

                    Don't ever mess with this man.
                    Ever.

Guard 2 lets go of Guard 1 and activates the barrier lift, so the car can go through.

                         GUARD 2 (CONT'D)
                    (in Chinese, to Dr Reth)
                    Please go ahead. Sorry for the
                    trouble my comrade gave you.

EXT. PORT - SUNRISE

As a golden sky opens the day, Ellis wakes up. Next to him, NI YU YI, a delicate and refined young Chinese lady in her mid-20s, and wearing a traditional Chinese dress, looks at the horizon through a suicide barrier.

                              ELLIS
                    You?

                              NI YU YI
                    Remember that place?

                              ELLIS
                    I barely remember last night's
                    party and how I ended up here.
                         (beat)
                    How could I ever forget this
                    place? Except for the suicide
                    barriers all around. They were
                    not there before.

NI YU YI
You were going to jump into
this poisonous soup not so
long ago.

ELLIS
We could say you saved my
life... even though I might
have survived.
   (beat)
Don't ask me why, please.
You helped change my mind
so I didn't jump. That was
something in itself.

NI YU YI
I was just being --

ELLIS
-- Yeah. Exactly. Just being
like those female characters
from Ancient Chinese stories
that my parents used to tell
me.

NI YU YI
A traditional woman.

ELLIS
Yes. I've never met one
in person before. Prior
to that point, I thought
those characters were pure
fiction or something from an
unreachable past. But meeting

you made all those stories not only even more relevant, but true, in a heartbeat. Proving that there are still humans that kind, that soft. The contrast was just too great to bear at first. After meeting you, I remembered that I lost interest in finding a wife, because I'd basically need to go back in time to find her. Or find you, which would be possibly harder than the first option.

              NI YU YI

I might have stopped you from jumping that day, deterred your course of action to live miserably with a woman that was not in sync with your deep-down values, but you lost your way again, didn't you?

              ELLIS

Yes. To make some sense of this world, I started on a less probable route: looking for you. But the only thing I found, again and again, were those legends.

              NI YU YI

Legends?

                    ELLIS
          Legends about you and others
          like you. Goddess-like women,
          preventing people that are
          about to take their own
          life right at the edge of
          risky zones all across the
          world. Hearing about them,
          in different versions,
          with different words and
          intonations, brought me great
          comfort.

                    NI YU YI
          But it was not enough to make
          you hang in there.

Ellis looks at the horizon, without
answering.

                    NI YU YI (CONT'D)
          What about some training?

                    ELLIS
          Beg your pardon? You almost
          sound like you would train me.

                    NI YU YI
          You can read minds?

                    ELLIS
          What? Why? I mean. For real?

NI YU YI
After your first mission, I'll find you.

ELLIS
Wait. After my first mission? One usually resumes one's training before beginning any action. It doesn't make any sense.

NI YU YI
Exactly Ellis, it does not, but it is all we have. Have you experienced anything that made sense recently?

ELLIS
Touché.

NI YU YI
Many people have put their life on the line to buy you some time, including Dr Reth.

ELLIS
Almost killing me in the process.

NI YU YI
Without his intervention, you would already be in the field as CCP cannon fodder. I will meet you after you accomplish your mission.

> ELLIS
> This is a Disposable Agent mission. It is highly probable --

> NI YU YI
> -- It is highly probable you won't make it. I know. But you have to try.
> (beat)
> Just be in the same mindset as when you decided to face that giant bullet.

> ELLIS
> You were...
> (beat)
> Actually, I don't really want to know.
> (beat)
> What about your name?

> NI YU YI
> My name?

> ELLIS
> Yes. What is your name? You know, small talk. I need to train in that too. Simple questions without the probability of a bizarre revelation or consequence.

A stunning futuristic and luxurious car pulls up in front of them.

PAX, 60, looks and acts like he is 50, has short curly hair, and a face showing an uncanny lack of concern for this era and wrinkles that command respect, opens the car door and steps out.

Ellis puts himself in front of Ni Nu Yi to protect her.

                    MAN
My name is Pax.

                    ELLIS
I don't recall an appointment with anyone having that name in the middle of nowhere.

                    PAX
Remember the prescription you received from Dr Reth? I am the therapist he mentioned. And this is... Well, my office for the day. Very soon, it will be your car.

                    ELLIS
I was kind of in the middle of... And you should know that I'm not a car guy. You didn't need to --

                    PAX
-- Totally aware of that! But just come here for a moment.

Pax invites Ellis to stand in front of the car and pops the hood.

> PAX (CONT'D)
> Beauty is only skin deep.
> (to Ni Yu yi)
> Except you, Ni Yu Yi.

Ellis looks at Ni Yu Yi.

She raises her eyebrows and looks at him with a smile.

> ELLIS
> (looking at the motor)
> Is it what I think it is?

> PAX
> You still have some attachments that keep you here in this lowly world.
> (beat)
> Yes, a car running on free energy. I saved it for you just before they trashed it. They prefer we continue to be dependent on them, but they made an exception.

> ELLIS
> And why did I get this free pass?

PAX

I've learned how to soften your heart. They were impressed. So I negotiated the car. Come on, get in!

He throws the keys for Ellis to catch. Ni Yu Yi is already gone.

ELLIS

You have figured this out too, right? Me... Her...

PAX

Cracked...Yes. But with good intentions. Not for them. Just give it some time. She'll find you when this is over.

ELLIS

Can this really be over with? By the way, is it your idea to have my training after my first mission? I still want to congratulate the one that had this brilliant idea.

PAX

Usually, you wouldn't have any training.
(beat)
Not giving proper training is part of their training. Their way to balance the odds so you have a fair

chance at accomplishing your mission as well as having a high probability of getting yourself killed in the process—or after. If you succeed in at least one mission, or even part of it, their investment was worth it. With her training, you will have some buffer to beat them at their own game, but the only way is to do it after the first mission.

                    ELLIS
I assume we are not being recorded right now.

                    PAX
We're not. But we will have to record a long boring conversation that will compensate later. A replacement tape.

                    ELLIS
   (sarcastic)
Sounds like fun.

                    PAX
It's not, actually. But necessary in these circumstances.

Pax receives an alert on his smartphone.

                    PAX (CONT'D)
          (laughing)
     Great! Just to make it worse,
     we are heading for a zone of
     imminent earthquakes and we
     have no way to detour.

                    ELLIS
     Canaries in the coal mine.

                    PAX
     Nothing is too dangerous
     for a Disposable Agent. Pre-
     apocalyptic surroundings with
     deadly sudden changes should
     be the least of your worries.
     You should even feel eager
     to experience them. The only
     thing to fear in this world
     is when and how the CCP will
     decide to inflict a new type
     of pain on you and how long
     you are able to bear it before
     you die.

Ellis looks at Pax for a few seconds
without saying anything.

                    ELLIS
     I couldn't have said it better.

Pax looks through his conductor window.

PAX
Looking at this world today, we can hardly see the difference between CCP destruction and Divine retribution. Plus, the CCP has acquired freaky weather control devices.

ELLIS
Why are you here in the first place? I never heard of a therapy session on-the-go that has a chance of dying trapped in a rock.

PAX
After I read a whole cabinet full of your files, I made sure I would be assigned to you.

ELLIS
I'm worth a whole cabinet? I'm touched. Failures take a lot of space to archive. If unimpressive is what rocks your world, knock yourself out!

PAX
It was more about the numerous missing pages in your reports... All those black - stripes obscuring sentences...

The nutty level of encryption of your digital files... I've never seen anything like it. And the penchant they have for your blood, I can tell you they are quite hooked on it. I know you are worth my time.

> ELLIS

You mean in a loser or a cuckoo way?

Pax and Ellis are shaken by some small seismic activity.

Pax hands Ellis a proper Disposable Agent handgun with the red light on.

> PAX

I wouldn't trust you with this if you were a first-class lunatic.

The green light engages the second Ellis takes the gun.

> ELLIS
> (looking at the gun)

I understand their value in this world, but you should know that I'm not a big fan of guns.

> **PAX**
> I do know that as well, but it is one of the requirements. You will find regular cartridges of bullets in the trunk. I've also selected for you some low-damage ammunition: rubber bullets, blank bullets, tranquilizers, and some other weapons that have not been tested yet. Without forgetting your future favourite. To tip the balance in a world full of lies.

> **ELLIS**
> Let me guess --

> **PAX**
> -- No time for that—truth serum darts.

Ellis tries to hide his smile.

> **PAX (CONT'D)**
> Moreover, you have a considerable amount of fire power back there. I've even provided some rounds that could take down a dinosaur.

> **ELLIS**
> Are you saying that this car could blow us up at any second while driving on these lovely

road conditions, but thanks to you, we are safe if we run into a T-Rex?

                    PAX
          I might have put a bit too
          much much care into your supplies.
               (beat)
          Where is your phone?

                    ELLIS
          Here.

Ellis hands over his smartphone box and Pax takes it and throws it out the window.

                    ELLIS (CONT'D)
          What's your problem?

Pax hands Ellis a flip phone. Ellis tries to open his window trying every button without success. Then, he tries to open his door, but it is also locked.

                    PAX
          This will help you be more
          focused. You won't be able to
          use that app of yours. You
          know, the one you developed
          clandestinely that reminds
          people to keep their hearts
          beating.

ELLIS
On second thought, it was a great idea for you to fill the car with explosive materials.

PAX
I want you to learn to extract beauty from ruins.

Pax and Ellis feel some mild earthquake tremors.

ELLIS
I believe that you are not the type of person who gives immediate reassurance when people are with you. You convinced me it will grow over time, right?

PAX
Hahahahaha! Soon, I assure you, you will desperately miss this precise moment we are having. Sure, we can be swallowed up at any moment by landslides or exploded to pieces flying in all directions --

ELLIS
-- Or both.

                    PAX
          But still, you will live this
          scene again and again in your
          head, wishing someone had let
          you know to savour it.

Ellis tries to stay unmoved while
dealing with some low intensity tremors.
He finally takes the phone from Pax's
hand and the earpiece that goes with it.

                    ELLIS
          What is your role in all of
          this?

                    PAX
          Helping you to bite the
          bullet.

                    ELLIS
          Would you mind being more
          explicit?

                    PAX
          It's an old expression.
          When doctors were short
          of anesthetics or during
          a battle, they would get
          patients to bite a bullet to
          distract them from the pain of
          being operated on.

                    ELLIS
          Good old anesthesia days...

                    PAX
Normally, my job is to assure
Disposable Agents have a
clear mind and heart, but
just the right amount, only
what it takes to achieve
their mission. If you throw
a bottle full of dirt into
water, it sinks. If you remove
the dirt, it will float up.
But they are very specific,
they don't want us to make
you float. Communists love
their Disposable Agents to not
be completely balanced. They
recommend keeping them in a
low-emotion level, and then,
keeping up a healthy death
rate among them.

                   ELLIS
But the rebel part of you
just wants to make us stellar
individuals, make us totally
float.

                    PAX
No. I want you to fly.

A massive landslip starts under the
car, which propels it in the air for
a few seconds. The car rolls over and
stabilizes on its wheels with, somehow,
almost no damage.

ELLIS
And, of course, it landed on its paws.

PAX
I really need to stay in my office. We are almost at McCarran International Airport. You can drive me there first.

ELLIS
You forgot to say please to your chauffeur.

PAX
We'll discuss your death wish, your parents, and how you will deal with your future's past in our next session. In my office in downtown Washington D.C.

ELLIS
Discuss my future's past? Hearing that would scare the living daylights out of anyone...

PAX
(uncomfortable)
Hahahahaha! Forget about that last part. Let's start with a lighter topic: your dress code.

ELLIS
You gotta be kidding me.

PAX
This is more a favour than a specific rule from the CCP.

ELLIS
We have slid quite quickly into the favour territory.

PAX
That's the pacing in this day and age, dear.

ELLIS
At the point that I am now...

PAX
Mr. Yan Cai Luo. Does that name ring a bell?

ELLIS
Nope.

PAX
He is a Chinese designer of Han couture.

ELLIS
Good for him. But I'm not in the fashion industry. But I doubt he is --

FLASHBACK: Ellis recalls all the intellectuals of America who were captured and died in an explosion in the Capitol Hill building.

> **PAX**
> -- He is still among us. He was hidden during the Capitol Intellectuals Massacre. He is well and alive with his wife, an Italian designer.

FLASHBACK: CCP agents enter the world's most famous museums containing classic artwork. Each time they attempt to raid one of them, they arrive too late. All paintings, sculptures, and valuable human art are gone... Each CCP agent is very angry about that happening, in his own unique way.

> **PAX (V.O.) (CONT'D)**
> He is the one that said to save most of humankind's classic works of art from destruction by the Chinese Communist Party as they invaded the world.

> **ELLIS**
> (amazed)
> So the rumour was true. The art was saved away.

> **PAX**
> He is the Monument Man of modern time. He's a big fan of

what you have done with that app of yours.
(beat)
Glad to have your attention back.

ELLIS
(smiling)
Go on.

PAX
One of his dreams was to co-create, with his wife, a half Han couture, half European collection.

ELLIS
Better late than never.

PAX
He is looking for a model.

ELLIS
Flattered, but it means I would be even more exposed, vulnerable, and an easy target. Plus, carrying a gun when they have been banned. That would be... perfect. It is time people started to pay tribute to him. It is the least I can do.

PAX
(excited)
You will make him so happy. I'll coordinate with the couple so you get your clothes before every mission. You have their first creations in the trunk.

ELLIS
And, of course, you gave them all my measurements and you knew I would say yes. Not sure they would be happy you put their work at risk as you did.

PAX
From this point on, two parallel stories will unfold. Some children of the world will be told the one about an elementary school teacher who became a terrifying Disposable Agent who stole all of the children from their families. This Disposable Agent is more feared than the boogeyman, and as unstoppable and powerful as the CCP itself.
(beat)
The other story I will tell my children tonight will be about a man, so screwed up by the CCP, he was forced to outmatch himself in all domains, so

> he could screw the CCP back
> and free us all, including
> himself.

>   ELLIS
> My shoulders might have a
> limit to the amount of weight
> they can hold. You should know
> that.

>   PAX
> You have learned to bear so
> much already. You'll do just
> fine.

Ellis drives Pax to the airport main door.

He drives into the heart of Las Vegas with his new car, alone.

EXT. CASINO - DAY

Leaving his car with a valet, Ellis enters a high-end casino.

Inside, he passes all levels of decadence, as if going through different levels of Hell, from top to bottom.

>   ELLIS (V.O.)
>   (to Pax)
> What about the mission I'm
> going to do? Are you the one
> that will brief me on it?

PAX (V.O.)
Correct. According to the information I've received, you will be a hired gun for this one.

ELLIS
Cool.

PAX
In all probability, there will be someone you care about there. Eliminate a potential threat, an enemy of the state can be translated, in our words, to: we are about to lose an ally, a friend. They want to push you past our human boundaries.

ELLIS
Eliminating the slightest chance of overthrowing the CCP and losing some humanity in the process. Sounds like a plan.
    (beat)
Is there any way to actually fail that mission, you know, avoid killing and be killed instead?

PAX
Sometimes, there is no shortcut. Even if the members

of the Confederacy, including
the ones you have met, are
there to back you up and to
assure a silver lining to
every cloud, sometimes, you'll
be on your own.

                ELLIS
          Humanity's artwork is safe for
          now and the Confederacy is
          real. Not bad!

The further Ellis enters into the
endless wickedness that this casino
reveals every second, the more security
staff become interested in him.

Ellis arrives at a steel door with an
electronic lock that requires a numbered
password.

Security employees from all levels
slowly approach Ellis's location.

                ELLIS (CONT'D)
            (to Pax)
          Steel door. Password required.
          Would you...

Holding his flip-phone, Ellis takes some
pictures for Pax. He feels a bit ashamed
to be using this antiquated model of
phone.

                    PAX (O.S.)
I was working on that code
before you arrived... for
almost an hour.

                    ELLIS
It would have been simpler and
faster if you had provided me
some film, a semi-automatic
camera, and a red chamber.
Meanwhile, I can take, what,
three pictures max with this
old phone?

                    PAX (O.S.)
Already received the files.
You can take 3,400 pictures
of very high quality. And
without using the aggressive
5G network.

                    ELLIS
This phone sounds as dangerous
as the ticking time-bomb car
you offered me earlier.

                    PAX
Give us a few seconds. We
should have the password for
you any minute now.

                    ELLIS
Please take your time.
Security have watched me
since I put my feet in this

hellhole. I need to get used to dressing so fashionably.

PAX (O.S.)
Nah! It's your aura that was caught on tape. Try 3-7-7-3-9-0.

Ellis enters the code. An annoying sound of the error message alerts Ellis and all gamblers around. They start getting weirder looks from people.

ELLIS
Wrong number, darling.

PAX (O.S.)
Damn! The password has expired. This particular device changes passwords every hour. And it takes --

ELLIS
-- An hour to crack. We are going to have a bright future together. I can feel it.

PAX (O.S.)
The only person that has a real-time updating password is beyond the door. You would need to make her leave that location.

                              ELLIS
                    Oh, so I would need to gas
                    her out? With what? Maybe I
                    could try to find the electric
                    panels and play with them and
                    get lucky. Or I could tease
                    the fire alarm with some
                    bullets of mine?

Ellis raises his Disposable Agent
handgun equipped with a silencer and
aims it at a sprinkler in the celling.

Someone in the Security office sees
Ellis's move on a security camera and
manually shuts down the fire alarm
system before Ellis can shoot a first
round. Nothing happens.

Gamblers in the area start to panic.

A different VOICE gives Ellis a new
code.

                              VOICE
                    2-6-9-1-4-9

Security guards, from undercover to
the heavily armed ones, move closer to
Ellis.

Ellis enters the code.

A transparent bulletproof glass traps Ellis between the steel door, still locked, and the security personnel.

One of the guards opens fire on the glass, but the bulletproof glass doesn't shatter.

Ellis draws his weapon, but doesn't waste any bullets on the glass wall.

He turns around and re-examines the steel door.

                    ELLIS
          See? That wasn't so hard.

                    PAX (O.S.)
          How in the world did you
          figure out the code that fast?

                    ELLIS
          What do you mean? Is someone
          else on the line?

                    PAX
          This is a secure line. Only I
          have access to it.

                    VOICE
          This man on the phone doesn't
          deserve credit for the
          password.

Ellis hits his earpiece to get rid of Pax.

                    VOICE (CONT'D)
          No need for an earpiece for
          you to hear me or talk to me.

Ellis removes his earpiece, and puts
it in his jacket pocket, but the voice
continues.

                    VOICE (CONT'D)
          I'm not part of your side.
          Let's say I'm a third party if
          I may express myself that way.

While looking all around him, Ellis
notices a GREEN PLANT on a small table,
under the password entering device,
between the bulletproof glass and steel
gate. He looks around it, under its
leaves, inside the dirt, and under the
pot.

Security guards are still shooting
different weapons at the bulletproof
glass. It won't hold much longer.

                    ELLIS
             (to himself)
          They must have put a freaking
          chip in my head.

                    VOICE
          I would know if you had one.
          So no, you don't. Tracers are
          still there in your body but
          they are not emitting anymore.

                    ELLIS
So I'm hearing voices now?

                    VOICE
You could say that, but not
as a crazy person would. I'm
real, very real.

                    ELLIS
OK. Whoever or whatever you
are, I'll go first and thank
you. That bulletproof glass is
a relief.

                    VOICE
My pleasure.

                    ELLIS
But it will soon be a thing
of the past. Should I enter
the same password to open the
steel door?

While talking, Ellis starts to punch
the password he used earlier with the
exception of the last digit.

                    VOICE
You do that and all the
bullets flying in our
direction will go through you
and me.
    (beat)
You are about to kill him,
right?

ELLIS
That's enough. Who is talking?

VOICE
It is not really talking. Telepathy is what it's called. You waste your time using your tongue, lungs, vocal cords, and lips. Just express yourself as if you were thinking about it and I'll get it. I'm not dumb.

ELLIS (V.O.)
(telepathically)
Just don't tell me you are the plant right here... Please don't.

GREEN PLANT (V.O.)
See! Not that difficult. Don't look at me when you communicate with me. They might suspect something. Not everyone has that ability.
(beat)
Correction, every human had this ability but it atrophied over time. It was discovered decades ago, but nobody believes in science nowadays. It is kind of an old thing now. How can you not know that?

ELLIS (V.O.)
Can we not have a conversation about science breakthroughs? I don't need a crash course on reconsidering everything in the universe right now!

GREEN PLANT
I'm impressed how quickly you mastered telepathy. It's as if you were used --

ELLIS
-- May I please, have the second password to open that steel door?

GREEN PLANT
I cannot.

ELLIS
This must be a prank.

GREEN PLANT
You cannot kill him. He is --

ELLIS
-- I'm sure he has an important part to play. I will do my best to avoid killing him, but I cannot promise you anything. I hope you know I'm not lying. I want him to live as much as you do.

> GREEN PLANT
> You want him to live more than yourself?

> ELLIS
> That is an idea I'm considering.

> GREEN PLANT
> It sounds like you would sacrifice yourself for egotistical reasons.

Security personnel arrive with a giant drill and start drilling the bulletproof glass door.

> ELLIS
> I can make that person's life easier.

Ellis starts to enter the first password.

> GREEN PLANT
> What are you doing?

> ELLIS
> Opening the bulletproof glass.

> PLANT
> OK, OK!

The plant interrupts him before he completes entering the code.

                    PLANT (CONT'D)
7-5-7-5-3

                    ELLIS
          Ah come on! There is a missing
          digit...

                    PLANT
          Oh, Sorry. My bad. 5.

                    ELLIS
          Catch up later.

                    PLANT
          What about catching me now?

                    ELLIS
          Looking like an oddball
          shouldn't make much difference
          at this point.

Ellis picks up the plant.

The steel door opens and closes after Ellis and the plant enter the room.

He walks a couple of meters. As he arrives at another door, he starts to notice a smell.

                    ELLIS (CONT'D)
          Incense...

Having his gun in one hand and the plant in the other, Ellis opens the door in front of him. The door has images of the inside of a Buddhist monastery carved into it, with a variety of colors highlighted with gold.

Once inside, his arm holding the gun falls down, as does the gun.

He picks up the gun, and hides it in a fancy leather case inside his jacket. He puts the plant on the nearest spot he can find.

>   ELLIS (CONT'D)
>   (desolate)
>   No, no, no...

Ellis understands that this room is a well-protected small Buddhist temple. A prototypical and ageless MONK, in his Buddhist robe, is sitting in meditation, with a subtle smile on his face.

>   MONK
>   Soon, going outside the Three
>   Realms. Soon, beyond the Five
>   Elements...

>   ELLIS
>   I...

>   MONK
>   Save your breath, you will
>   need it.

ELLIS
You need to leave this place.
Is there any...

MONK
Before the invasion of the Chinese, this panic room was designed to protect crime lords, dictators, and people who committed horrendous offenses, many of which were on children... Now, we are considered more evil than all of them combined. There is only one way out. There was always only one way out. You need to leave --

ELLIS
-- I cannot leave here without --

MONK
-- I'm not talking about leaving that room. Consider your mission accomplished.

ELLIS
But you...

MONK
There is only one way out, and that's how you will leave too.

ELLIS
Can you at least reassure me that all that gibberish you said will make sense at one point?

MONK
It already does to an extent that you cannot fully process now.

A loud tinkling indicates to Ellis that the bulletproof glass door has broken and that the troops are at the steel door.

After a long silence, the door Ellis entered starts to melt, melding the colors and gold together.

ELLIS
What the...

MONK
Only a blessing in disguise.

ELLIS
They ordered me to take your life...

MONK
That won't be necessary.

Ellis looks for another exit.

MONK (CONT'D)
The invisible and the intangible are the Dao. The visible and the tangible are only the packaging. A quote from *The Book of Changes*.

ELLIS
Will this help me find an exit to get you out of here?

MONK
No. It was just to annoy you more. No door here other than the one that has started to liquefy.

Ellis takes the gun and puts the barrel to his head.

Ellis receives a call from Pax. Ellis puts the earpiece in his ear.

PAX (O.S.)
I was hoping you wouldn't resort to this. Bad news, pal. You cannot terminate yourself with your service weapon. In a certain range, you cannot shoot yourself. You can ask someone else to do it, but as you know, your weapon only activates with your fingerprints.

The monk cannot hide his laughter.

Ellis touches his earpiece to hang up on Pax.

The door is almost totally melted now.

Ellis puts himself in front of the monk and waits with his gun pointed at where the first person will enter.

> MONK
> I'm going to ask you to look at the Buddha statue and focus on it.

> ELLIS
> But the door...

> MONK
> Put the gun down and try to focus on the Buddha statue as long as you can.

Ellis takes a moment and faces the Buddha statue.

He immediately hears someone pull a pin from a grenade but the sound is in slow motion.

> MONK (CONT'D)
> Keep concentrating.

The pin from the grenade hits the floor, slowly echoing.

> MONK (CONT'D)
> Keep going.

Still in slow motion, the resonating sound of a grenade hitting the floor after rushing through the hole in the door is heard.

Ellis focuses himself on what the monk asked him to do. He closes his eyes.

A huge flash saturates the whole room with light.

> MONK (O.S.) (CONT'D)
> You did just great. He expects you soon as well. But some things need to be done first. Whatever brought you to the verge of death all these times has never been your disinterest in life, but a misplaced anticipation of what is coming next. Don't let impatience finish you off.

A huge energy wave erupts from the monk, propelling everything in slow motion, including everything in the room (except Ellis), everything and everyone in the casino, and everything within a radius of 20 miles around the casino.

Back to reality. Ellis opens his eyes.

                    SKYE (V.O.)
          Nothing beats a flash grenade
          to make an introduction.

A CCP investigation team is in the room,
along with Skye.

                    SKYE
               (to Ellis)
          Mission accomplished, agent!
          Even if you sought trouble
          right off the bat by wearing
          those fancy clothes, it didn't
          affect your performance.

The monk is sitting in the same position
as before the blast and looks like he is
alive; but Skye feels no pulse when he
puts his fingers on his neck.

                    SKYE (CONT'D)
          Without using a bullet on top
          of that. Obviously, someone
          is looking for a promotion to
          work his way up.
               (beat)
          You are expected.

                    ELLIS
          Expected?

                    SKYE
          Even I don't have the
          clearance to know more.

Skye grabs Ellis and puts a black cloth bag over his head.

INT. DARK ROOM - LATER

The monk's body is cremated in a glass crematorium, under the eyes of some SCIENTISTS and Mo Hong Long. After cremation, the scientists pick up small shiny pebbles from the monk's ashes.

> SCIENTIST
> (in Chinese)
> Sarira, once again, Sir.

> MO HONG LONG
> Continue researching them.

A few glass jars on a table next to them contain hundreds and hundreds of sariras (pearlized or crystal-like bead-shaped objects found after cremation of enlightened monks).

> SCIENTIST
> Mr. Shortliffe was delivered to the hallway leading to your office as requested.

> MO HONG LONG
> (laughing, in Chinese)
> His last name gets me every time.

ACT 3

INT. HALLWAY - DAY

A hand removes the sack from Ellis's head and pushes him into a very narrow hallway museum.

The same hand closes the door behind Ellis and locks it.

The hallway leads to sumptuous double doors, the ones that only an emperor could have commissioned. Before the doors, plastinated human bodies without skin, from the famous *Body World* exhibition, line both sides of the hall in glass cases. Each corpse seems utterly terrified about what is behind the double doors.

The doors open by themselves as Ellis approaches. They reveal a very luxurious office with another door visible on the other side of the room.

Mo Hong Long turns around to face Ellis. He is behind his desk.

The doors close behind Ellis once he enters the office.

                    MO HONG LONG
          Mr. Shortliffe. Please have a
          seat.

Ellis looks at him and sits without a
word.

                    MO HONG LONG (CONT'D)
                    (smiling)
          Don't bother saying anything.
          I know what is on your mind.
                    (beat)
          And that is dully predictable.
          Everyone has the same thought.
          But I'll give you the rare
          opportunity of making it a
          reality.

Mo Hong Long points to a box on the
table in front of Ellis.

Ellis opens it: a loaded antique Chinese
gun awaits him. After a few seconds he
closes the box.

                    ELLIS
          It could never be that
          easy. This would inevitably
          turn against me or others.
          Moreover, you cannot kill
          communism with a bullet. Even
          if you aim at its big head.

> MO HONG LONG
> What's the point of destroying communism when no one believed in it in the first place, not even us? Not even me. There are things worth fighting for, and this is not one of them.

Through the door Ellis entered, a man storms in, gun in hand, ready to kill Mo Hong Long. He looks identical to... Mo Hong Long.

The original Mo Hong Long draws his own antique Chinese gun and lethally shoots the man.

The Mo Hong Long copy falls down.

> ELLIS
> What the heck...

> MO HONG LONG
> This? It happens all the time. At this precise moment, not only does the whole population but even most communist party officials want me to step down.

Two copies of Mo Hong Long rise up from the floor, both aiming a gun at the original Mo Hong Long.

The original avoids all bullets shot at him and then shoots and kills the "clones," as well as a third one that entered from a side door of the office.

The original Mo Hong Long reloads his gun.

> MO HONG LONG (CONT'D)
> But as you see, whatever the number, this is pointless. I'd even say: "Bring it on!"

Many copies of Mo Hong Long enter by the other office doors and try to shoot the real Mo Hong Long.

"Clones" that were shot to death rise from the floor, but always double in number, until the office is packed with copies of Mo Hong Long, including the original still standing. All are engaging in a mini-war; but the original Mo Hong Long has the upper hand.

While the office is a battlefield, Ellis picks up the gun in the box and ducks behind a chair, waiting for the carnage to end.

When peace returns, Ellis opens his eyes. Every copy of Mo Hong Long is pointing a gun at him.

He sits on the chair while slowly putting his gun back in the box.

> MO HONG LONG (CONT'D)
> But at one point, the killing fades. Enemies become allies. New supporters added in. Temporarily.

> ELLIS
> What is this all about?

> MO HONG LONG
> Showing you what would happen if you had the courage to do the right thing.
> (beat)
> Nothing! Hahahahaha! Like the term of that presidency, there is no end in sight.

> ELLIS
> Even today, there are people who still believe that there is no such thing as pure evil.

> MO HONG LONG
> Most don't believe in pure goodness. So they cannot conceive of the complete opposite.

A few dozen of the Mo Hong Long copies start to sing, harmoniously like a choir.

MO HONG LONG (CONT'D)
(in Chinese)
"The old society turned humans into ghosts, the new society turned ghosts into humans."

"There has never been a saviour of the world, nor deities, nor emperors on whom to depend. To create humankind's happiness we must entirely depend on ourselves!"

ELLIS
Some folks out there still think your worst crime is not what you do to the flesh, it is severing your link with the Gods.

MO HONG LONG
Going against the Gods was only the preliminary stage, as socialism was to communism.
(beat)
We have made sure that the Gods abandoned you slowly. This process started a few centuries ago. Humans progressively lessened their thinking about doing good. They considered good to be a silly and outdated attribute. Until something at a higher

realm takes charge and cleans up the mess.

> ELLIS

So no heaven on earth as promised by your mass-killing predecessors?

> MO HONG LONG

It has been a heaven on earth for the very few of us and we have made sure to keep it that way.
>   (beat)
> We have recently put our hands on hidden technologies that can transform our civilization as we know it: the ability to make deserts green, to desalinize ocean water, to generate free energy, to eliminate radioactivity, to eliminate pollution... We have the means to sustain far more people than are presently on the planet, we have anti-gravity, limitless clean energy, amazing health technologies that can eliminate all the problems and diseases we have, speed up healing --

ELLIS
-- Why make things easy on us, right?

MO HONG LONG
Mankind is still not ready for these things, and even more so, is not worthy of having them. We are the guardians. Making sure you don't annihilate yourselves too quickly so you can experience the worst punishment of all.

ELLIS
Why are you keeping me alive?

MO HONG LONG
Outside of the fact that you have been caught in a Faustian kind of wager with me and myself, you will spread terror as one of us.

ELLIS
What makes you so sure I will comply?

MO HONG LONG
Anything you say or don't say about what you have just experienced will crush anyone's morale. You have been soaked in just enough

maleficence to spread it around.

> ELLIS
> Anyone could have done that job.

> MO HONG LONG
> True, but no one raised the bar of excitement to unparalleled levels like you did.

One of the Mo Hong Long clones put the black bag on Ellis' head.

I/E. BLACK

Ellis is being transported by car, but unable to see anything. The brakes are suddenly applied hard.

> CHINESE THUG 1 (O.S.)
> (in Chinese)
> Why are we stopping now?

> CHINESE THUG 2 (O.S.)
> (in Chinese)
> Did you see that? She just...

The sound of something jumping on the car resonates inside.

> CHINESE THUG 1 (O.S.)
> How can she...! Just drive. Forget what you saw. Don't even

mention it. You heard what
they do to anyone who mentions
supernormal activities in
their report.

          CHINESE THUG 2 (O.S.)
Yeah. I still have bits of
that guy on my uniform. Just
because he talked about a
super-cat.

          CHINESE THUG 1
Shhhhhhhhhhhhh!!!

The sound of glass breaking, fist fights, and gunshot pops here and there until a car door is opened.

Ni Yu Yi removes the black bag from Ellis's head.

EXT. ROAD - DAY - LATER

The Chinese thugs in army clothes are unconscious on the road next to the van that was transporting Ellis. There is spectacular damage to the vehicle.

          NI YU YI
   Too bad you missed the show.

          ELLIS
    (disoriented)
The sound effects were
terrific!

EXT. ROAD - NIGHT

Ni Yu Yi drives Ellis's car.

They enter a very rocky part of the former United States.

> ELLIS
>
> Where...

> NI YU YI
>
> You wouldn't believe it if I told you.
> (beat)
> You would literally not believe me until we arrived at the site even if I spelled out in detail where we are heading. So I'll skip the explanation. We are close.

> ELLIS
>
> How can you --

> NI YU YI
>
> -- Read minds?
> (beat)
> The process of human thinking is a very slow one. I can tap into your brain and process your thoughts before you do. Totally unintentional I might add, before you ask.

ELLIS
You seem able to even determine the different outcomes of a train of thought. Kind of cool... if you were doing it to another person.
Any other person.
   (beat)
And now you let me talk but I am kind of repeating myself to you, aren't I?
   (beat)
Is there a way you can shut this off? It's like I am mentally naked. But in a way it forces me to be more mindful about the nature and quality of my thoughts.

NI YU YI
Don't worry. I understood long ago that most of our thoughts are not what we really are. Purity and innocence are the essence of a being. I taught myself to ignore the rest, cut me out of it.

ELLIS
And you were just making an exception for me? Is it "All thoughts you can read Day" but no one told me?

NI YU YI
(genuinely amused and laughing)
Sometimes, in extreme circumstances. I can be distracted, so I focus on different things and forget to switch it off.
(beat)
What plant are you thinking about? Telepathy?

ELLIS
(surprised)
Oh! I was just putting what happens now on a mental list of weird things that have happened to me recently. Just pretend that I didn't... think anything.
(beat)
Wait... That day when I passed out, you were not only reading my thoughts, you were in there with me, right?

NI YU YI
Yes. That was a first. Uncharted waters for me.

ELLIS
At least another person believes me now. But kind of boring to talk about during a nice dinner when compared

to someone that is reading thoughts.

          NI YU YI
This is something I never asked for or was looking for. Let's say it is maybe a side effect of the different travel I've been doing. This Dharma Ending Period is quite a fascinating one.

          ELLIS
Is that how you find which person in a crowd is about to take their own life?

          NI YU YI
Yes.

          ELLIS
All the bruising suicidal thoughts you must have listened to...

          NI YU YI
It is even more painful to listen to passive suicidal thoughts. Most humans have them constantly.

          ELLIS
Black pill thoughts?

                NI YU YI
Yes.
     (beat)
Sadly, we have always been
outnumbered when it comes to
helping those who are ready to
end their life.

                ELLIS
Is everything you have
mentioned part of the
training? Should I stop
somewhere and pick up a
notebook?

                NI YU YI
The training started eons ago,
Ellis.

                ELLIS
Hahahahaha! More far-out talk.
     (beat)
I think it will be simpler for
everyone if I just nod at all
the eccentric stuff I hear.
Training started eons ago.
Nodding.
     (in a compassionate tone)
Did the CCP ever know about
that power of yours?

Ni Yu Yi doesn't answer. Ni Yu Yi fights to keep a placid face.

                    ELLIS (CONT'D)
          I'm sorry Ni Yu Yi.

Ni Yu Yi drives into a cavern where they can hide the car.

EXT. ROCKY DESERT - NIGHT

Ni Yu Yi walks with Ellis for a few minutes before they enter another cave that slopes down. Ni Yu Yi lights up a flare that she holds in her hand.

INT. CAVE - NIGHT

Going first, Ni Yu Yi puts a foot on a crumbling rock that causes her to tumble into the cave.

Ellis tries to grab her hand but misses.

She performs a very artistic somersault, a Chinese classical dance move. She then lands as light as a feather on the flat rock in the cave.

She picks up the flare from the ground, still offering its light to them.

Looking at the rock floor, Ellis notices some greasy black deposit under his feet that lead to many burned out flares.

In front of them, there is only a rock wall.

                    NI YU YI
               (looking at the flare, she
          says to Ellis)
          Wait for it, wait for it...

As the flare fades out, the flat rock wall in front of them gradually reveals a transparent glowing light—a hidden portal.

                    ELLIS
          You know I won't even think
          about going through there.

                    NI YU YI
          Yep! As if you had mentioned
          it to me years ago.

                    ELLIS
          Hahahaha! Really? Let's
          explore the free will option
          first.

Ellis turns around and starts to leave the cave.

EXT. ROCKY DESERT - NIGHT

With his head half out of the cave, Ellis sees three drones equipped with a video camera and a flamethrower, doing surveillance rounds and toasting the interiors of nearby caves.

Ni Yu Yi enters the portal slowly. Her voice now comes from it, with a mystical echo.

                ELLIS
     (to Ni Yu Yi)
  They have tracked us.

              NI YU YI (O.S.)
  No. I've encountered those drones before. I thought the same thing at first, but I've been told that the drones are doing rounds in remote places where people can hide and transition from one part of the world to another.
     (beat)
  I've also learned that Chinese tech only works once out of every two tries and that the solar storms we experienced recently have destroyed many of the existing satellites, including theirs. So the chances of being followed are extremely low.

              ELLIS
Is there any requirement for entering that portal, such as having a pure heart and if not...

              NI YU YI
Not having a good heart will get you pulverized to the

smallest particles still
unknown to man.

     ELLIS
That brings great comfort.
Thanks!

     NI YU YI
Hahahahaha!
 (beat)
I understand you don't want to
enter, but in order to survive
here, you first have to go
through it.

Ellis looks at the night sky and stars through the mouth of the cave.

Suddenly, a drone arrives at the cave entrance and shoots all the fire it has into the cave, without noticing Ellis back away just in time.

As he goes deeper into the cave to hide, he gets closer and closer to the portal. The flame hitting the floor of the cave explains the black streaks he previously noticed.

While thinking about going through the portal, he realizes the light from the flames has shut down the portal. He sees only a regular rock wall.

The fire moves deeper into the cave, forcing Ellis to back up to the rock wall.

Just as the fire is about to burn his skin, Ellis hears a loud meowing.

The drone is immediately attracted to it and leaves Ellis in peace.

The portal reactivates.

Ellis turns and begins to enter.

POST-CREDIT SCENE

The three drones are on fire, throwing flames at each other and flying in a circle, until they crash, one after the other, at Adriel's feet.

Adriel turns toward the cat that seems to be returning to its original form, not shown on screen.

Adriel bows to it respectfully, following the ancient Chinese custom.

<u>END OF PILOT</u>

www.ingramcontent.com/pod-product-compliance
Lightning Source LLC
LaVergne TN
LVHW041637060526
838200LV00040B/1607